London on my Mind

London
on
my Mind

CLARA ALVES
TRANSLATED BY NINA PERROTTA

PUSH

Originally published in Brazilian Portuguese in 2022 as *Romance Real* by
Seguinte/Editora Schwarcz SA, São Paulo, © 2022 by Clara Alves

Copyright © 2022 by Clara Alves

English translation copyright © 2024 by Nina Perrotta

Library of Congress Cataloging-in-Publication Data available

ISBN 978-1-339-01489-0

10 9 8 7 6 5 4 3 2 1   24 25 26 27 28

Printed in Italy   183

First edition, June 2024

Book design by Maithili Joshi

Browser window throughout © Shutterstock.com

For anyone who has always been denied
the leading role in fairy tales.

I hope you can see yourself in this story
and dream of your own happily ever after.

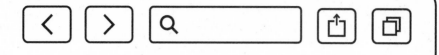

A Royal Affair?

by Chloe Ward

The Duke of York has some explaining to do. Sources say Prince Arthur has been meeting with an as-yet-unidentified woman. At the Royal Ascot race on Saturday, Queen Diana's son was seen slipping away to a private room, accompanied by an unknown woman—despite having arrived at the event with Tanya Parekh, his wife of almost ten years.

"Arthur's been acting rather odd. He sneaks out of the palace and gets caught in unusual places for a member of the royal family to be, and last week everyone overheard a heated argument between him and the duchess," revealed a source close to the couple.

It seems we mere mortals aren't the only ones plagued by infidelity. On the contrary: Royal relationships are marked by controversy, the most well-known being the late King Oliver's betrayal of his then-wife, Queen Mother Daisy.

But the story of Prince Arthur and Tanya Parekh has been sold to us from the beginning as a real-life fairy tale. Could it be that our Prince Charming is really a frog?

Chapter 1

The jet engines roared as the little light turned on over my head. I tried to look out the window, but the shade was almost all the way down and the person sitting by the window was asleep. How anyone can sleep with all the noise and turbulence of the plane constantly reminding them that they're miles off the ground, I'll never know.

My grandma used to tell all kinds of stories about airplane travel in the late 1900s, and it had always seemed so glamorous.

But there was nothing glamorous about flying.

The seat was too small, and I spent a good part of the trip with my stomach squished by the tight seat belt until a flight attendant noticed how uncomfortable I was and offered me an extender. Seriously, why don't they inform fat people they have extenders at the beginning of the flight?

I'd picked the aisle seat because I didn't want to bother anyone when I had to get up—I have a tiny bladder, so it was bound to happen. But I'd forgotten that sitting at the end of the row meant people would inevitably bother *me*.

Plus, the bathroom was small, and I barely managed to keep my balance squatting over the toilet, trying to keep the pee from running down my leg.

When the wheels finally touched down, making the plane bounce and the bags rattle in the overhead compartments, my heart almost jumped out of my mouth. All I could think about was getting home and taking a shower.

Except I wasn't going home. And I wouldn't be going home for a long time.

I forced myself to file that thought in the Things I Can't Think About or I'll Freak Out folder, then pulled on my backpack as I waited for the line of passengers to start moving down the aisle. I waited while sitting, obviously, even though sleepyhead over by the window and the woman between us—who had spent so much of the flight typing on her laptop that I could still hear the clickety-clack of her keyboard—were already standing, leaning on the seats in front of them, as if every second they waited cost ten years of their lives.

Now would be a good time to turn my phone off airplane mode and let my grandparents know I'd arrived safely. They were probably anxious, waiting to hear from me. But I didn't even take the phone out of my bag. I still couldn't bring myself to talk to them.

When the line started moving, I waited for the aisle to clear before standing up, instead of trying to squeeze between the passengers. I could feel two pairs of eyes glaring at me.

Personally, I wasn't in any rush to get off the plane. As bad as the last twelve hours had been, I knew they were a lot better than what was waiting for me outside.

Unfortunately, as the line shrank, I had no choice but to follow the last passengers toward the metal staircase that would bring us down to the tarmac, where we'd have to take a shuttle bus. In that moment, frozen by the cold wind of the gray city before me, even though it was the end of spring, I had a shocking realization:

I hated London.

Never in my life did I think I'd say that. But there's a first time for everything, right?

To be clear, I've always loved England, and ever since I became a One Direction fan, I've dreamed of visiting the United Kingdom. (I know, I'm a walking cliché—I also love reading fanfiction while drinking coffee at Starbucks and wearing my hair in a messy bun.) I loved the cold. I loved the fact that the city had a café on every corner. Every time I thought about going to London, my chest tingled with excitement. And even if One Direction was on an indefinite hiatus, I still dreamed they would announce a comeback conveniently during my visit, with one of those huge shows at Wembley Stadium and, who knows, maybe even a meet-and-greet. If I was lucky, I might even run into Harry and Louis (my favorites) just walking around!

But now the city represented my new life. Everything from my daily routine to the most important things had stayed behind in Brazil: my friends, school, grandparents, my mom—or, to be precise, the *memory* of my mom. The couch we used to lounge on, watching telenovelas. The corner of the table where she always sat to talk with clients and take orders. Her bed, which I climbed into all those nights when I couldn't sleep. Everything that reminded me of her had stayed behind with the life I loved.

Of all the bad things about my move to London, though, the worst was the irritating little man waving at me through the sliding doors of the arrivals gate: Roberto, my dad.

I hadn't seen him in over ten years, but there was no mistaking him. Roberto's exaggerated gestures were just like mine; our thick, curly brown hair differed only in length (his was shorter, while mine came down to my shoulders); and the smile he gave me was the same one I saw in the mirror.

Not that I felt like smiling just then. He didn't seem to care about that when I stopped beside him, pushing a cart with my bags.

"Wow, Dayana! Look how you've grown!" Roberto held me by the shoulders to admire me, as if who I'd become was all thanks to him. "Gosh, I can't even believe you're here!"

He was so excited, all his sentences ended like this! Full of exclamation points!

That two-faced dirtbag seemed to have forgotten that he'd abandoned my mom and me ten years earlier to seek his fortune abroad. Which meant that, at seventeen, I'd spent more of my life not seeing that man's face than I'd spent with him.

Of course, he hadn't disappeared completely—my mom would never have let him live it up in Europe while she struggled to raise her daughter alone. He sent money when things weren't "too difficult" and called on special occasions, like Christmas and my birthday.

But that was it.

Just that.

Nothing like fatherly love.

A small, vengeful part of me was glad he was being forced to fulfill his parental role after so many years of neglect. But mostly I was consumed by the painful losses that just kept piling up. How was I supposed to live with this man and look him in the eye every day? The man who had abandoned me when I was still a child and started a new family in a different country? The man who greeted me with a smile at the airport, as if we were really father and daughter and not two strangers?

I didn't reciprocate his enthusiasm. I clenched my jaw and squeezed the cart's handle harder.

"Yeah, I can't believe I'm here, either," I replied through gritted teeth, but he didn't hear the bitterness in my voice, or pretended not to. He just grabbed my backpack, took the cart, and walked me to the parking lot, talking about how excited he was to see me and how he couldn't wait to show me around London.

So that was it, then? After ten years of neglect, he had nothing to say? No apology? No *I'm sorry for everything that happened?* No *Your mom died, but I'm here for you now?*

All these questions started to bubble up inside me as if I were a bottomless pit of hatred and anger. I wanted to turn into a volcano and spew my rage everywhere, without worrying over who might be in the line of fire. I'm proud to say that I managed to hold it together for the whole car ride. At least until we parked in front of a small white row house.

That was when I found myself face-to-face with two smiling women—a mother and daughter standing in the doorway, looking at me full of fake anticipation, as if I were in London for vacation. As if we were one big happy family.

"Hiii, querida," Lauren said, switching between Portuguese and English.

I was barely up the front steps when Lauren's shrill voice hit me and I was pulled in for a hug. She led me inside with one arm around my shoulder while her daughter, Georgia, who still hadn't said a word, followed close behind.

"It's so great you're here! We're so excited to have you! You're going to love Londres!"

Roberto came up behind us, dragging my heavy bags.

From the backyard, a bark announced the presence of Ruffles, probably the only creature in this house that I would get along with. I'd seen the Scottish terrier in some of our (very rare) video calls, and my dad mentioned him now and again, but I'd totally forgotten he existed as I wallowed in self-pity at the thought of the move.

"This is your room."

Roberto put my bags in the bedroom next to the living room, but I didn't have a chance to follow him and take refuge there because I was still trapped by Lauren's arm, forced to listen to her chatter about how perfect London was.

I had talked to Lauren a few times on the phone. My mom and I used to laugh at the pretentious way she mixed English and Portuguese, and we'd make fun of the false note in her voice when she talked to me like we were best friends. As if I hadn't heard her pushy whispers on the other end of the line when my dad took the phone to ask if I needed anything. Anything material, of course, because that was all he could offer me.

Because Lauren was so obviously fake, our inside joke back home was to call her "Lauriane"—the Brazilian version of her name.

I should have been amused to meet Lauren in person. I should have been holding back laughter at her endless monologue. I should have been taking mental note of all the things I would tell my mom on the phone later so we could giggle about her together.

But I didn't do any of that.

First, because I didn't think this was funny at all.

Second, because there wouldn't be a phone call to my mom later—or ever.

So no one can blame me for exploding all of a sudden, when Lauren, like an insensitive, crap-spewing fire hose, started talking about the trips she was planning for us, including to Disneyland Paris.

"Could you just shut up?!" I yelled so loud it scratched my throat.

I twisted out of her grip and stood facing her.

My dad had just come back into the living room, and his footsteps stopped dead, along with every other sound in the house. Even Ruffles stopped barking, leaving the room in total silence. Everyone looked at me in surprise.

"I don't want to go to Disneyland! I don't want to live in London! I don't want anything to do with this crappy family!"

I almost stomped my foot at the end—that's how frustrated I was—but I didn't want to seem like a spoiled little girl, so I controlled myself.

"Dayana! Watch how you talk to Lauren!" my dad said, serious for the first time since I'd met him at the airport.

I turned to him and was struck by the stern expression on

his face. But even his intimidating gaze wasn't enough to stop me.

"I'll talk however I want! Who do you think you are to boss me around? You have no right to tell me what to do."

I saw the exact moment when he broke. His posture stopped being so threatening; his eyes darted from me to Lauren, and then to his stepdaughter, who had been silently watching the whole argument with raised eyebrows. He opened his mouth to respond but then closed it without saying anything. And that gave me the strength to continue:

"You abandoned us, you disappeared from my life, you never wanted to know a single thing about your own daughter, and now that I'm o-bli-ga-ted"—I spoke slowly and clearly—"to come here, you want to act like a father? Give me a break!"

"I . . . You don't . . ." he stammered.

Before either of us could say anything more, Lauren cut in:

"We won't allow this kind of behavior in this house, Dayana."

Her face was serious, her voice harsh. She ruled with a firm hand, just like my mom did. But she was a cheap imitation of the person I loved most in the world, the person who was no longer in my life. Maybe that's why, against all reasonable expectations, I started laughing. I laughed loud and hard, to the point that tears ran down my cheeks. I laughed so much I had to bend over, holding my bruised stomach.

Eventually, the laughter died from my lips and the tears stopped flowing. Instead of replying to Lauren, I just looked her up and down and then turned to Roberto.

"So that's how it's gonna be? The whole family teaming up against the intruder?"

"Dayana, let's not talk about this right now," he pleaded, visibly frustrated.

I didn't know how to read the expression on his face. He seemed wounded, but that was impossible: He didn't have the right to feel hurt. My mom and I did.

Not him.

Never.

Since I didn't want to keep looking at the pain in his face, I stomped to my new room and slammed the door so hard the walls shook. My legs were wobbly, as if I were back on the plane, miles up in the air, far away from solid ground.

The sound of the keys jingling to the rhythm of our steps was like music to my ears. My mom and I headed down the hallway to our hotel room. I skipped ahead, eager and smiling, turning back only to say, "Come on!"

Behind us, my dad carried all our suitcases, leaving us free to walk down the hall as if we were two fancy ladies. My mom must have somehow charmed him into taking the bags, but I was too excited to notice.

Mom caught my eye and gestured toward Roberto, then gave me a little smile.

"You see, Day?" Dad said. "You're Superman's daughter."

I giggled.

"He looks more like the Hulk to me!" Mom exclaimed.

We both laughed. Dad glared at us.

"Hey, I can hear you! You better be careful with the Hulk."

The key slotted into the lock of our hotel room. I could barely wait for Mom to open the door before pushing past her and running inside.

"Wow, look at this bed, Mommy!"

I leaped onto the bed and started jumping before my parents had time to stop me. As I soared toward the ceiling, I turned to face my parents—but instead of disapproval, I saw only tenderness in my mother's eyes.

"How is it?" she asked. "Good for jumping?"

"The BEST!" I said, panting.

Dad appeared in the doorway, dropping our bags all at once.

"Careful with my suitcase!" Mom scolded.

"You're the ones who should be careful—the Hulk has arrived!"

He spread his arms wide, his hands in the shape of claws, and started chasing us, grunting, as we ran shrieking around the room.

Laughing like a happy family.

Chapter 2

I didn't respond when Roberto came to call me for dinner. My door didn't lock, but he didn't dare open it. I couldn't help overhearing Lauren threaten, in her high-pitched voice, to come get me herself, but my dad whispered something that convinced her not to.

I didn't leave the room even when my stomach started grumbling. Somewhere in my bag, I still had a little pack of cookies from the plane, and that was what lined my stomach while I waited for the exhaustion of the trip to knock me out.

My body was begging for a restorative night's sleep, but my head was going one hundred miles per hour. I stared at the textured paint on the ceiling until the house fell silent. I thought everyone was asleep, but after a while, I heard someone come downstairs and open the front door. I was curious, alert to the smallest sounds, and that kept me awake. I spent some time stalking the members of One Direction, trying to figure out if they were in London, but I didn't find anything. Their profiles hadn't been active since their hiatus. Then I put on some of the band's old videos, which kept me occupied until I heard the front door open again hours later. Overcome by my thirst for gossip, I opened my door a crack, as silently as I could, in time to see Georgia tiptoeing up to her room. So the beloved daughter wasn't so perfect after all, was she?

My curiosity satisfied, I finally gave in to sleep.

I dreamed of laughter and happy families and woke with a start, a lump in my throat. It took me a while to realize I'd been woken up not by the dream but by a warm tongue licking my hand, which was hanging over the side of the bed. A cute little dog barely more than a foot tall, with reddish spots in his white fur, looked happily up at me while he drooled all over my hand.

Behind him, Lauren was standing in the doorway in her pajamas, holding the doorknob and calling my name.

"Breakfast!" she said when she saw I was awake.

I grumbled and turned toward the wall, pulling the comforter over my head. I felt like a tractor had run me over, reversed, and then crushed me again. How long had I slept? It felt like it hadn't even been ten minutes.

"I'm not hungry."

"Hunger strikes are absolutely prohibidos in this house." Lauren pulled back the comforter. "Get up," she insisted when I scowled at her.

I sat up in bed, still grumpy, but it did the job. She left the room with a satisfied smile, giving me some time to wake up. Ruffles stuck his snout under the covers.

I rubbed my eyes with my dry hand, trying to blink the sleep away. The room started to come into focus. It wasn't that big, but there was also basically no decoration to fill the space. The walls were white but looked like they'd seen better days. To my left was an old wooden wardrobe, the only piece of furniture in the room besides the twin bed against the right-hand wall and the nightstand next to it. I'd spent so much time analyzing its details the night before that the room was etched into my mind, as if it had always been mine.

The thick comforter that covered me smelled strongly of fabric softener. My sheets in Brazil had also smelled like fabric softener, but it was different. It was the smell of fabric softener that *my mom* had chosen.

The smell of home.

I still hadn't unpacked. My two suitcases lay open on the floor, their contents completely jumbled from when I dug out my pajamas, ruining the careful packing I had done to fit everything I owned inside.

I looked at the terrier.

"Do you mind if I tell your owner to go to hell, Ruffles?"

He wagged his tail.

I just wanted to sleep in peace, but peace wasn't something I would have in this house.

With a sigh that was both a way to vent my frustration and an attempt to gather my strength, I got out of bed and went to drink my beloved coffee.

Lauren was in the kitchen, humming while she made pancakes. It was a long room, with the entire left side taken up by counters and shelves. Georgia was already sitting at the table to the right, looking like a zombie.

At least I wasn't the only one in a bad mood about being woken up too early.

Or maybe her sulky expression was caused by a hangover. I remembered how clumsy she had been when she got back from her little nighttime excursion.

I washed Ruffles's drool off my hands and sat next to my new little sister without a word.

"Bom dia, Dayana," Lauriane greeted me as she turned around with the frying pan, as if she wasn't the one who had woken me up.

"Good morning," I mumbled when I realized she was waiting for a reply.

God, what an unbearable woman.

"There's café." She nodded at a canister of instant coffee on the table. "And água quente for tea." She pointed at the electric kettle in the sink. "And I made pancakes."

She flashed a wide, toothy smile as she transferred the pancakes to a plate in the middle of the table.

Then she stood there looking at me.

"Thank . . . you?" I offered with a shrug. It was the right thing to say, because she went back to the stove for another round of pancakes.

Georgia didn't say thank you. She just grabbed a pancake with her hand and started eating it.

My fake sister was a year younger than me, but we were going to start the second year of high school together. Since I hadn't finished my school year in Brazil and classes in England didn't start until September, the principal thought it was best for me to start over. I was far enough behind already because of the differences in curriculum between the two countries. So yeah, really exciting . . . I could hardly wait. I would make a point of picking as many different classes from Georgia as possible. Judging by her surly expression, I didn't think we'd be walking around school arm in arm.

Roberto appeared just as I came back to the table with my coffee. He cheerfully wished us good morning, kissing the tops of our heads as if last night's argument hadn't happened at all.

Was everyone in this family born with their heads up their butts? It was the only explanation for all of them acting like one big happy family with zero problems, despite us having yelled at each other just a few hours earlier.

Further proof of my theory was how relaxed Lauren and Roberto seemed when they talked about the barbecue they were planning for lunch to celebrate my arrival.

After breakfast, Roberto headed out to buy meat and Georgia mumbled that she was going back to bed because she "wasn't feeling well"—so my hangover theory was right.

I thought that was my cue to escape to my room, but of course I was ambushed by the insufferable Lauriane.

* * *

"I can't believe I came all the way to London just to be exploited," I murmured when I got within earshot of the kitchen, where Lauren was starting to prepare lunch.

Ruffles stood beside her, dying for a distraction.

I pushed the vacuum through the living room full of dog hair with a fury that barely fit inside me.

"There's no exploitation in this house, amor. Everyone does their part aqui." I could hear Lauren clearly over the noise of the vacuum.

From where I stood, I could see her through the doorway between the two rooms. She was wearing a sweatshirt and had pulled her sleek, dark red hair into a bun. Physically, Lauren was the odd result of a marriage between an Englishman and a Brazilian woman: She had curly brown hair that she straightened and dyed, but she also had light skin and blue eyes. She had a long nose, her thin lips pursed in a severe expression. She wasn't pretty, exactly, but she wasn't ugly, either. Certain parts of her face just looked kind of disproportionate.

I turned off the vacuum and leaned on it as I stared Lauren

down. "Your daughter must be really useless if the only way she can help is by sleeping."

Lauren ignored my jab and continued her speech. "And while you're living here, you'll have to get used to taking responsibility and respecting your elders."

I raised my eyebrows. "I don't know how long it's been since you were in Brazil, but there they teach us that respect should be mutual. Is it different here in Europe?"

I smiled sarcastically and got an irritated look from Lauren in return. Her blue eyes were a little scary when she looked at me like that, but maybe because of everything that was happening, I didn't feel intimidated by my stepmother. I must have lost my sense of danger.

"We won't tolerate any more outbursts like the one you had yesterday, okay?" she warned, finally being direct with me. "We know you're going through a hard time, but your father and I have welcomed you with open arms, despite your rebel-without-a-cause attitude. You'll have to learn to adapt, whether you want to or not."

I didn't know what to say, so I turned the vacuum on again to avoid the sound of her voice. I turned my back to her and headed toward the front hallway.

I knew I couldn't go back, obviously. I wasn't welcome in Brazil, not anymore.

Swallowing the lump that had formed in my throat for the second time that day, I went upstairs and started furiously vacuuming the second-floor hallway. It was a small space with three closed doors. I approached them one by one, going out of my way to ram the vacuum into each door a few times. When I got to the third door, the one that faced the stairs, it suddenly opened.

Georgia stared at me with her face scrunched and her curly hair tangled.

"What the hell are you doing?!" she shouted in English, her voice hoarse with sleep.

I shrugged, putting on my best poker face.

"Sorry, I don't speak Stupidese," I said, but it came out with a ridiculous accent that annoyed me.

Even though my English was advanced—I'd passed a proficiency test and everything so I could enroll in school here—my speaking skills were embarrassing. If British schools were anything like the ones in the movies, I'd definitely be bullied for my inability to pronounce English words right. I'd be the Brazilian laughingstock of the entire school.

Georgia took a deep breath.

"I was resting," she said in perfect Portuguese, and I wanted to die.

I'd talked to Georgia a few times on the phone, but only when she was the one who happened to pick up—which she always did in English. As soon as she heard my Portuguese, she started yelling "Daaaaad!" really loud, without even answering me. Since I knew she'd grown up in England, I figured she'd never learned the language.

But considering that her mom and stepdad were Brazilian, and that Roberto didn't speak English that well even after living in London for ten years, it made sense that she knew Portuguese.

She just never wanted to talk to me.

"I'm cleaning the house." I shrugged. Learning this about Georgia in my current state of annoyance made my cheeks burn with rage. "Your mom told me to."

"And do you need to break down the doors to clean?"

"Sorry to interrupt your rest, Your Majesty. I'll try to be a model servant from now on."

She looked at me with a mixture of anger and pity. Then she opened the door all the way and gestured toward her room.

"You can clean in here, then. Now that I'm up."

I stomped into the room. Who did she think she was to boss me around? Was that why they let me live here—because they needed a maid? Was this how my life was going to be now?

As I grumbled under my breath, Georgia went back to bed. I watched her out of the corner of my eye. I'd been so irritated by yesterday's move that I hadn't had time to pay any attention to her. I mean, I'd seen photos of her on Roberto's Facebook, but this was the first time I'd stopped to really look at my new little sister. Georgia had inherited pretty much nothing from her mom: She had very dark skin; thick, slightly lighter lips; dark brown, almost black, eyes; and curly hair that fell in tight ringlets around her face. Although I had no idea what her father looked like—all I knew was that he was also Brazilian and that Georgia hadn't even started to walk when he left, a few months before she and Lauren moved to England—she could only be an exact copy of him. The only things she seemed to have gotten from her mother were her high cheekbones and sparse eyebrows.

She looked terrible, and I wondered if maybe she was telling the truth about not feeling well. But then I dismissed the idea. She'd gone out secretly and woken up the next day feeling bad—did she think I was born yesterday?

Georgia leaned back against the wall, pulled her legs up on the bed, and rested her head on her knees, watching me vacuum. I made sure to keep a surly look on my face. Sick or not, it wasn't fair that she was just sitting there while I cleaned.

After a few seconds of silence, she sighed.

"I know you hate our dad," she burst out when I turned in her direction, "but he's a good person."

I pretended not to hear.

I kept vacuuming close to where she sat, under the desk and by the door.

"He hasn't stopped talking about you since he found out you were coming."

24

I could sense she was still watching me, waiting for a reply. But it was easy for her to defend him. To Georgia, he was an ideal father. To Georgia, he'd given his all.

"You know I was abandoned by my biological father, too, right? And Roberto didn't think twice about adopting me . . . even though he didn't have to."

"No," I agreed, finally responding but still not looking at her. "Roberto's responsibility was to raise *his own* daughter. I think we can agree that he doesn't seem to like dealing with his responsibilities."

"You're being pretty unfair. I know he made mistakes, but at least he's trying to make up for it. At least you still have a chance to have a father."

I shut off the vacuum but didn't turn around.

Unfair. That was the word I'd heard most in the last few months.

"Yeah, maybe," I said quietly. "Maybe I'm being unfair for not forgiving the man who was my hero, who was my best friend, who told me he was going to England to give us a better life and then never came back. Maybe I'm being unfair, but considering everything that's happened, I think I have the right to be."

Without looking back, I left the vacuum where it was, ran down the stairs to my room, grabbed my bag, and left that suffocating house.

"What a stupid idea, Beto!" My mom's nervous laughter filled the room, even with the door closed. I stopped coloring the fish in my coloring book and raised my head to listen. "When you mentioned going to England, I thought you meant for a vacation, not to live there!"

England? Wasn't that, like, really far away? How would I go to school and see my friends if we were far away?

"Ah, meu amor," Dad sang, in that playful, charming way that always persuaded my mom. "Weren't you the one who wanted to live in the land of royalty?"

Oh, the land of royalty! That was where Lady Di lived, and Princes Arthur and Andrew. It must be pretty cool . . .

"But, Beto, that was just a pipe dream. Maybe if we didn't have Day . . ."

Hey! She wanted to go to the land of royalty without me? So unfair! I almost got up to open the door and complain, but before I could make up my mind, my mom went on, "How will I manage there on my own? I can only work here because my parents help out. They take her to school, pick her up, and even spend time with her during the day. If we go to England, there won't be anyone to support us."

"I know, but things are too hard here, amor. I'm having trouble getting back into the job market." He lowered his voice, and I had to sneak to the door and open it a crack to

26

hear him. "Mara was telling me about a friend of hers who's doing well there. Apparently, the minimum wage is almost six pounds an hour. If I work at least forty hours a week, I'll make almost a thousand pounds a month! That's enough for me to get by there and send some money back for you two. The British pound is almost three Brazilian reais! The cash will pile up in no time."

"Wait—you're thinking of going alone?" Mom was mad now. And I was, too. I didn't want Daddy to leave us.

"Just until I'm set up there. I'll go first, to find a job and a place for us to live, and I'll send money home. When everything's ready, you and Day can join me."

My mom said nothing for a long time. Then she sighed. "I don't know, Beto. I need to think. Can you give me some time? You've done your research, and now I need to do mine."

"I thought you knew everything about England," he joked, trying to lighten the mood. "The country where Muse comes from—aren't they your favorite band? And that sappy movie you love. And your inspiration—Diana!"

My mom laughed. She seemed to soften.

"Well, maybe it's not such a bad idea. I'll think about it, okay?"

She left the room, and I closed the door as fast as I could. I ran back to my table and looked at the unfinished picture, my heart pounding.

Hmm, England. It was far away, but they had kings and queens there, princes and princesses. I really wanted to see a princess, and I could invite my friends to come visit. I hoped my mom would say yes.

Chapter 3

London had always been a shared dream.

My mom's favorite movie was *Notting Hill* (she even had a VHS version, which was just decorative, of course, but she displayed it with pride on the TV stand), and we'd watched the movie so many times that I knew the words by heart. I didn't even like it that much: It was old, the script was kind of weird, and Hugh Grant's awkwardness annoyed me, but I loved the London setting as much as my mom did.

On top of that, we were both obsessed with the royal family, and not just the current one. We watched all kinds of movies and shows—historical and contemporary—about the British royals, and we kept up with all the news and scandals. Royal events were a special occasion at our house. We made fish and chips and spent the whole day in front of the TV, watching the live broadcast.

It also wasn't a coincidence that I was named Dayana. Obviously, I wished my mom hadn't Brazilianized the name of the Queen (who at that point was still a princess), but she said the change gave me my own special charm. Lady Day, she used to call me.

My mom went through a pretty dark time after she and my dad split up, and for a while she hated everything having to do with England. We couldn't even use English words. I had to call the mall the centro comercial, hamburgers became sanduíches, and even email was now correio eletrônico. We couldn't watch movies or shows in English, not even if they were from the US. We had a long phase where we only watched Brazilian and Mexican telenovelas, and even K-dramas. And if I wanted to play a *single* English song? Don't even think about it! She almost threw out her precious autographed Oasis albums.

And then one day, after watching an inspirational Spanish movie that bored me to death (but made her cry like crazy), she decided that the mourning period was over, and she wasn't going to give up the things she'd always loved on account of that "cowardly jerk." So I was free to like England again.

Which was lucky because, otherwise, I wouldn't have discovered One Direction, and my life would've been a big empty void.

Since her death, though, I hadn't had the courage to look up any news about England. I hadn't even watched the coronation of Lady Di—now Queen Diana—after King Oliver's death. Those kinds of things were too painful because every little detail reminded me of my mom.

But in that moment, after leaving my dad's house with no destination in mind, after a full day of feeling mistreated, unwanted, and abandoned, I found myself taking the London Underground to the place my mom and I had always dreamed of seeing.

Buckingham Palace.

Its solid, old-fashioned architecture rose up before me with a kind of majesty, just as I'd expected. From the square in front of the palace, where there was a monument to Queen Victoria, I could see the full length of the rectangular three-story building, protected by a wrought iron fence and the traditional guards with red uniforms and tall, furry hats. I knew that the square was surrounded by the trees of St. James's Park. If I turned and headed in the opposite direction, I'd reach the Tudor-era royal residence. But I was hypnotized by the building in front of me. I felt a sudden thrill of excitement. It was the beginning of June, which meant the palace wasn't open to visitors, because the Queen still hadn't left for her summer holidays.

Would I catch a glimpse of the People's Queen someday? Diana had always been a global icon, even when she was still a princess. Not just for her simple elegance, which was too modern for the traditional outfits of British royalty, but also for her beliefs. When rumors started to spread that Prince Andrew, her eldest son, was gay, Diana was the first member of the royal family to support him. She told the papers she didn't understand why there was so much fuss about Andrew's sexuality, and she was offended that they would ask what she thought about it or whether it made her uncomfortable. Why would she be uncomfortable? Her son was still the same person, regardless of his sexual orientation. A month later, when Andrew actually did come out as gay, she stood by his side, holding his hand.

Rumor had it that Diana's husband, Edward Mitchell, wasn't happy about this—nor was her father, King Oliver. A few months later, she separated from her husband and threatened to break with the royal family. She was the king's only daughter, and a rift between them would disrupt the line of succession. So King Oliver resolved everything with donations to LGBTQIAP+ organizations and a declaration that the royal family was against discrimination in all its forms.

Diana was really incredible.

My mom would be out of her mind with excitement if she knew where I was.

The thought hit me like an arrow, and my stomach dropped. I pushed the image of her away and started to walk around the palace, listening to my One Direction playlist.

Suddenly, I heard "Infinity" fade into "Diana." My heart was pounding, but the heavy chords drowned it out as I followed the palace fence toward a side street. It was nearly evening, but the sky was still light. I knew the days would get longer and longer as we approached the solstice. The previous day, the sun had set after nine.

Even so, the streets around the palace were quiet. Most of the tourists stuck to the square in front of the main entrance, and there weren't any businesses nearby, just some buildings in the same architectural style as the palace—old and imposing, all cream-colored, clean, and light—though I didn't know what any of them were for. A building under construction rose up on the next corner. As I walked, I noticed a banner tied to the palace fence announcing that the Queen's Gallery was temporarily closed.

A movement behind the fence caught my eye just as "Diana" stopped playing: I was getting a video call from my grandparents. I'd talked to them briefly the night before, but it still felt terrible having to face them. The move had been my idea, but I couldn't help feeling that they'd betrayed me by letting me go so easily. They were the only real family I had left, and still they didn't think twice before sending me off to my dad's house.

Aching at the thought, I ignored the call.

And guilt immediately started to eat away at me. *You deserved to be sent off like that,* said a little voice in my head.

When the call disappeared from the screen, I noticed that I had a bunch of messages and missed calls from Lauren and Roberto. I ignored them, too. I pressed play on the music and put the phone in my pocket, but before I could start walking again, the banner next to me started to sway dangerously, as if caught in a hurricane. Only it wasn't windy at all.

I looked up in time to see a figure jumping over the fence to my right, heading straight for me. I fell down, and the two of us rolled on the ground in a tangle of arms, legs, and hair. My headphones detached from my phone and the music stopped again.

I was about to start cursing at full volume, but I'd barely gotten a word out when someone behind me covered my mouth. In that moment, I put two and two together and arrived at an alarming four. I had such bad luck that I'd run into a robber on my first day in London—and he was fleeing the palace!

What should I do? Is he armed? Oh my god! Will he kill me because I saw him escape?

My mom had always taught me not to fight back if I was mugged, but in the heat of the moment, logic doesn't matter. I started writhing, my scream muffled by my attacker's smooth palm. Then the person let go, allowing me to turn. I suddenly realized that my assailant was, in fact, a woman.

A *young* woman.

And really pretty.

"I'm so sorry. I'm so, so sorry," she said in English. "I didn't see you there. There's no need to yell."

She kept talking, but I wasn't listening anymore.

She was quite tall, though maybe it just seemed that way because I was still on the ground. Her red hair was partially tied back, but the fall had pulled half of it free, and the copper strands traced the right side of her face down past her chin. She was slim and had a sort of rebellious vibe, the look of someone who's ready to start a fight. But, judging by her clothes, she was far from being a bad girl: She wore a starched gray long-sleeved dress that went down to her knees and low-heeled shoes. Now that I thought of it, her outfit was much too uncomfortable for the risky stunt she'd just pulled.

She reached out to help me up, and I frowned. Was she actually a robber after all? With manners like that? If not, why had she run from the palace and jumped the fence like a bat out of hell?

I wanted to ask her, but then I heard hurried footsteps coming toward us. Her eyes widened in alarm. I looked back in time to see, through the metal bars of the fence, two men in suits leaving the palace and running out to the street. From the fear on her face, I could guess who they were looking for.

Then, without thinking, I grabbed her hand.

"Run, dammit!" I yelled in Portuguese, and we took off down the sidewalk.

She didn't think twice about coming with me. My unplugged headphones bounced against my jacket, silent now.

We crossed the road when the traffic let up for a second, then slipped down a side street and disappeared from view. We bumped into a few people, but there was no time to say sorry.

While we were running, she turned to look at me.

"Are you Brazilian?" she asked in Portuguese. I was so surprised that I stopped dead, and since we were holding hands, we both almost fell.

Wait, what?

"You speak Portuguese?"

She definitely wasn't from Brazil, or Portugal, or anywhere else where Portuguese is the main language; or, if she was, she hadn't grown up there. Her question was weighted with a strong English accent, but she clearly had some level of fluency.

Now this was a coincidence!

I stood staring at her, still in shock, and suddenly I was swallowed up by the bright green irises that met my gaze. I was intensely aware that we were still holding hands and that her long, slender fingers were interlaced with mine. I blushed, and a smile played around her delicate lips.

Before I could respond, she looked over my shoulder and squeezed my hand.

"I'll explain later," she said, in English this time.

I looked back, too, and saw that the men in suits were still on our trail. I started running again, without really knowing where to go, but she guided us, turning so many corners and taking us down so many alleys that I was totally lost. We blended in with the crowd and crossed a few avenues. I saw a red double-decker bus pass by and was momentarily stunned: It was the iconic London bus.

We were on a long, busy street when I noticed a Starbucks sign. I looked over my shoulder again, checking that the men still hadn't turned the corner, and pulled the girl inside. We headed toward the back of the store, where the cash register was, in hopes of disguising ourselves among the customers.

Or maybe because I wanted to seize the opportunity to get to know her better.

We got in line, trying to both catch our breath and shield ourselves from anyone looking through the window. As I snuck a glance toward the street, I accidentally met the girl's eyes. We laughed conspiratorially, as if we'd known each other for years.

Once we'd sat down at a table tucked away in a corner, disposable cups in our hands, I finally said, "So . . ."

To which she responded, "So . . ."

A smile formed on my lips, and I took a sip of my chai latte to hide it. She had a hoarse, deepish voice, the kind that gets into your soul and echoes inside you. Her green eyes examined me.

"Do you speak English?" was her first question.

I was expecting a *Why did you help me?* but this was better. If she'd asked that, I wouldn't have known what to say.

I moved my hand uncertainly, in a gesture that meant *more or less.* "And you speak Portuguese."

She imitated my gesture. "My mom is Brazilian," she said, taking a sip of her iced matcha. "I learned Portuguese as a kid, but I only ever practice with her. It's a hard language."

She spoke Portuguese with a cute accent and some English words sprinkled in, but unlike Lauren, who seemed to think her coarse way of mixing the two languages impressed people, the girl only used English when she didn't know how to say something.

"It is, sometimes even for us," I agreed. Then, realizing we still hadn't introduced ourselves, I added, "My name is Dayana, by the way."

"Bloody hell!" she exclaimed, and I wondered if I'd said something wrong. "Mine too!"

"No way. Are you messing with me?" It was my turn to widen my eyes in disbelief.

She frowned, probably unfamiliar with the slang I'd used. I laughed.

"I'm just surprised," I clarified, my mind still reeling at all the coincidences in this odd situation. "But do you spell yours like the Queen?"

She shifted in her chair, looking uncomfortable. "What do you mean?"

I pulled out my phone, opened the Notes app, and typed my name. I turned the screen toward her. "Mine is spelled like this."

"Oh! No, mine is . . ." She took the phone from my hand and typed *Diana*.

"Just like the People's Queen," I said again.

This time she understood, but she only nodded.

Did she not like the royal family?

The thought reminded me of how we'd met, and I couldn't help turning the conversation toward my biggest question.

"Why were you running away?"

I tried to seem casual, but my words were brimming with curiosity.

She took a long drink of matcha before shooting back, "Why did you help me?"

Well, she had me there. I didn't know what to say.

We smiled at each other, aware that both questions were too personal for a first conversation. But we were also aware that there was something between us, a bond that had formed when I'd grabbed her hand.

I wasn't sure what had prompted me to help her. Not her pretty face, though that had definitely caught my eye. Under the yellowy glow of the Starbucks lamps, her ginger hair seemed to give off a light of its own, and the dimple in her right cheek stood out beneath a layer of freckles. She was like an otherworldly being—a fairy from old English folklore.

Maybe helping her had been my way of rebelling against London.

Helping this girl escape from the palace of the *Queen of England* herself was the biggest act of resistance I could think of. And I was pretty damn pissed at England right then.

A ringtone interrupted our eye contact.

Diana pulled her phone from her pocket, looked at the screen, and sighed. "I think I have to go."

She didn't seem very convinced. My whole body tingled with curiosity, but I didn't ask any questions. Instead, I held out my phone.

"Can I have your number?" I asked, anxious and unsure of myself and terrified she'd say no. My heart was racing.

Diana hesitated.

"I can help you practice Portuguese, if you want," I pressed.

If she hesitates again, I'll just leave it.

Diana took my phone with a little laugh.

"What is it you say in Brazil? A promise is a doubt?" she asked in Portuguese as she stood up and handed me the phone. I pressed my lips together, trying not to giggle at the way she'd mixed up *doubt* and *debt*, nodding with as much seriousness as I could manage. "And thank you. For the help. I needed it." She smiled and picked up her half-finished matcha. "Text me."

With a wave, she left.

I bit my lip, feeling strangely content for the first time since I arrived in the UK.

I plugged my headphones back into my phone and opened Spotify.

"Diana" was still paused.

I smiled.

Maybe London wasn't so bad after all.

"Mom, where are you? It's starting!"

I straightened my tiara and heard her steps come slowly toward the living room.

On the TV, the "Wedding March" started playing. I jumped onto the couch in excitement.

"What is that?" My mom laughed, eyeing the outfit I'd chosen specially for the occasion: Prince Arthur and Tanya Parekh's royal wedding.

Besides the plastic tiara, I was wearing a white romper and holding the flowerpot filled with my mom's lilies.

"I'm practicing for my royal wedding."

I got up and paraded slowly around the room, as if walking into a church.

My mom put some fries on the coffee table. Her eyes were swollen, but it was because she was tired, I thought. I was so hyped-up that I didn't notice her lack of enthusiasm.

"I don't think there are any royals your age, are there?" she said, her voice weak.

I pouted. "There isn't a prince who's my age?"

She gave me that familiar look of maternal tenderness. "I don't think so, my little princess. Not unless one of them has a long-lost son out there somewhere."

I collapsed onto the soft cushions with no elegance whatsoever, resting the flowerpot on the right arm of the couch.

"Ugh. I hope they find a long-lost son for me to marry

42

before we move to England. Do you think Daddy can intro-
duce me to the Queen?"

My mom laughed faintly and turned to look at the TV.

I didn't know it yet, but England was no longer part of
the plan.

Chapter 4

How long should I wait before texting someone? Was the same day too soon? Or should I do what I wanted without worrying about that?

I had zero experience with dating, or even hookups, especially when it came to girls. My only relationship (if you could call it that) had been with a boy from school who I had a crush on for months before he even noticed me. And when things *finally* got going, he wouldn't tell anyone and insisted we keep it a secret. My friends said he was ashamed of me and that I should end things as soon as possible. But it was hard to convince myself not to accept scraps when the other option was being alone again.

Fate ended up deciding for me. Six months later, my mom died and everything in my life fell apart. I didn't care about anything anymore, especially not a boy who was embarrassed to be with me.

My current question was the kind of thing I'd usually ask my best friend, Emilly. She knew how to deal with girls—she was basically an expert. Emi had been with more girls than I could imagine, and she gave great romantic advice.

But I hadn't talked to Emi since my mom's funeral. Not to her or any of my friends back in Brazil. I hadn't had the courage to face them after what happened. I was too scared of seeing the judgment in their eyes.

So, instead of texting Emi, I just imagined what she would do. I could almost hear her saying, "Life's too short to be afraid of sending a simple hello." I took my phone from my pocket, opened WhatsApp, and typed *Hey, it's Dayana*.

My finger hovered over the send button.

The door of my room opened suddenly, and I jumped, accidentally pressing send.

"Dayana!" Lauren shouted. "Where have you been? We were so worried!"

I stared at the sent message, my heart almost jumping out of my chest. Then I turned to my stepmother. *Goddammit.*

"Ever heard of knocking?" I asked, irritated.

Lauren put her hands on her hips.

"Ever heard of calling to tell us you'll be home late? Didn't you see our chamadas?"

A smile almost stole across my lips, but I kept my face neutral and shrugged.

"Do I have to give you a full report on everything I do?"

Lauren pinched the bridge of her nose, as if trying to stifle her annoyance. I seemed to have a special talent for getting under her skin.

She took a deep breath.

"Come eat," she said, her voice serious.

As soon as she left, I let out the worst swears I knew.

My grandma said my mouth was too dirty for my own good, but what could I do? That was how my mom raised me. She said it was better to curse someone out than keep it all bottled up inside.

I took one last look at my message to Diana, but there was only one check mark, meaning she hadn't received it yet. I dropped the phone on my bed and headed to the kitchen.

Georgia sat quietly beside me at the table, and my dad faced me.

"Lauren says you went out today," Roberto said calmly as he filled his plate. "Did you get to see some of the city?"

My stepmother glared at him. This clearly wasn't what she had in mind when she told him about my escape. But what *was* she expecting? It was only my second day living with Roberto, and I could already tell how much he hated conflict. It wasn't a coincidence that he was acting like everything was fine between us. This was how he tried to de-escalate a tense situation—by pretending nothing had happened. As far as I could tell, my dad's philosophy was that time heals all wounds.

The problem was that *too much* time had passed for things to resolve on their own. In fact, they'd only gotten worse.

But I wasn't going to be the one to raise the subject. After all these years, I deserved the bare minimum: for him to *want* to resolve things between us. If he didn't want to, I wasn't going to worry about it, either.

At the same time, I couldn't just sit at the table and have a casual chat with him. There was too much stuck in my throat.

"Yeah," I said flatly, serving myself some coleslaw.

There was also a plate of grilled meat on the table. I remembered that my dad had planned on barbecuing to "celebrate" my arrival. Apparently, I hadn't shown up to my own welcome party, but even that hadn't annoyed him. This realization hurt my feelings even more.

"I went to the place my mom always wanted to visit," I added.

Roberto cleared his throat nervously and looked down at his plate. Lauren didn't dare scold me, and I brought my fork to my mouth, savoring the coleslaw. The strained atmosphere at the table gave me a perverse kind of pleasure.

The silence didn't last long. Lauriane started talking to Roberto about some nonsense, trying to dispel the dark cloud I'd created. I kept my mouth shut, ignoring her chatter and focusing on the clink of silverware against plates and the occasional bark from Ruffles in the backyard.

When I lifted my head to reach for my water glass, I noticed that Georgia was sitting completely still beside me. I glanced at her face and saw that she had the same weak, sickly look as before.

"Georgia, querida, is everything okay?" Lauren asked before I could say anything.

The girl shook her head slowly.

"What's wrong?" Lauren asked.

"It's that pain again. But it's worse now. I feel kind of nauseous."

Beads of sweat glistened on her forehead.

She must have gone pretty hard last night if her hangover wasn't better by now.

"I think I'm gonna throw up."

Georgia's face was contorted with pain as she walked gingerly toward the bathroom.

Lauren got up quickly to help her, and Roberto followed. Based on their worried faces, they didn't seem to have considered for a second that Georgia might be hungover.

The first time I'd gotten wasted, I'd ended up staying at Emilly's so my mom wouldn't suspect anything. But the hangover was so brutal there was no way to hide it, even the next morning, because I couldn't stand up without feeling sick. After that, I'd never wanted to drink again. God, what a miserable experience.

It seemed Lauren and Roberto were more easily fooled than my mom. A few minutes later, they were running around frantically, grabbing jackets, a purse, car keys. My dad rushed upstairs, and Lauren led Georgia, who looked like she was about to faint, to the front door. Ruffles, sensing the turmoil through the glass of the back door, barked even louder.

When mother and daughter had almost made it to the sidewalk, Roberto came downstairs, took the car key from the hall table, and turned to me urgently.

"Dayana, we're taking Georgia to the hospital. Wait for us here."

I nodded, too stunned to speak.

"Thanks. I'll see you later."

He hesitated for a moment, unsure whether to hug me, kiss me, or just leave. Finally, he came over and gave me an awkward pat on the head. Then he ran outside as if his life depended on it.

The house fell silent.

I just stood there for a minute, staring at the door.

Then, bit by bit, a feeling of loneliness started eating away at me.

I should be happy, right? It was nice being home alone— Lauren couldn't keep her mouth shut for a second, and her grating voice was like a bad song I couldn't get out of my head.

But being alone . . .

Being alone was worse.

The coleslaw had lost its flavor, and I started to clear the table, putting the pans back on the stove and piling the plates haphazardly in the sink. I opened the back door so

Ruffles could come in and keep me company, but that little traitor ran to the front door and stayed there, whimpering for his owners.

So I picked out a playlist and turned the volume way up, trying to muffle any unwelcome thoughts while I washed the dishes. When I'd finished cleaning up, I threw myself on my bed, anxious for a certain response.

But I hadn't gotten a single notification.

I pressed the buttons on the landline phone, barely noticing that I was crumpling the sheet of paper in my other hand. In the distance, I could still hear the shower running. My mom's address book was open on the hall table, the letter R *at the top of the page.*

Someone picked up. She had a soft voice and spoke English.

"Hello?" the girl said with a strong British accent.

I held the phone tighter.

"Hi," I said shyly. "This is Dayana. Can I talk to my dad?"

The girl didn't even respond. She dropped the phone onto some hard surface, making an uncomfortably loud noise in my ear, and yelled in the background, "Dad!"

I may not have known much English yet, but I knew exactly what Dad *meant.*

Father. Pai.

My hands were shaking. I looked at the drawing I was still holding: three stick figures standing in front of a house holding hands, with glued-on letters at the top spelling out Happy Father's Day.

But before my dad could answer, I hung up and ripped the drawing to pieces.

Chapter 5

No one said anything about the hospital at breakfast the next morning.

I'd gone to bed before they got home, but I could feel how dark the mood in the house was when Lauren woke me up, looking exhausted.

She and Georgia sat at the table in silence, which might have been normal for Georgia, but definitely not for Lauriane. Roberto had the same cheerful, laid-back vibe as always. Avoiding conflict.

Maybe because I was fed up, or because I hadn't slept well, I blurted out after a few minutes of silence, "So no one's going to tell me what happened yesterday? I thought we were all one big, beautiful happy family."

"Nothing happened, amor," Lauren said. "Georgia just wasn't feeling well."

Beside me, Georgia let out a strange sound, somewhere between a scoff and an ironic laugh. I thought she was going to start an argument with her mom, but she just rolled her eyes.

It seemed she was taking a page out of Roberto's book.

Lauriane, on the other hand, had a temper. Like me.

I shuddered at the thought.

"But that's really all it was, querida," she insisted, even though her daughter hadn't said a word. "Didn't you hear what the doctor said?"

"Of course I did," Georgia said through gritted teeth, just as I asked, "What did the doctor say?"

"It's none of your business," Georgia muttered.

I almost laughed when I realized my little sister was pissed at me. What a triumph! This just added fuel to my fire, which was already fed by a good mixture of anger, frustration, and hurt feelings.

"What do you mean, *querida*? Is that any way to talk to your sister?" It was as if every word chipped away at my sense of decency, freeing me to talk more and more. "I'm just worried about you. If even the doctors can't figure out the cause of a simple illness that coincidentally started right after you got home late, then it must be pretty serious."

That was when something terrible happened: Lauren agreed with me.

"See, amor? That's what I was saying. Even Dayana thinks so."

"Oh, okay!" Georgia stood up suddenly, her chair screeching against the floor. "Now Dayana's the expert, huh? It's such a relief that you both know *sooo* much about my body."

"Georgia, sweetie, calm down." Roberto reached toward her, gesturing for her to sit down. "You have to understand that we don't know what to do if the doctors tell us there's nothing to worry about. But we can find another doctor and try to get a different diagnosis. There's no need to fight like this."

"I'd love to understand that, Roberto, but it's pretty hard when my *entire body* hurts and no one seems to believe me."

I could see the sadness in his eyes when she used his name. It was like Georgia knew it would hurt him and was doing it on purpose. Still, he didn't let it get to him.

"We'll figure it out, baby girl, I promise."

He gave her a reassuring smile, which seemed to frustrate her even more. The fact that he'd called her baby girl had *my* blood boiling, too. He had some real nerve, saying that right in front of me.

I felt a sort of bitter satisfaction when Georgia shouted, "DON'T TALK TO ME LIKE THAT! I'M NOT YOUR DAUGHTER!" She pointed angrily at me. Ruffles, who'd been resting under the table, jumped with fright. "YOUR DAUGHTER'S RIGHT THERE! APPARENTLY DYING FOR YOUR ATTENTION."

Before anyone could respond, she stomped up the stairs so hard I felt the floor shake. She slammed the door of her room and let out a scream of frustration. Then the house fell silent.

Lauren and Roberto looked at me.

I stared down at my lap, wondering what I could say to get out of this situation.

"Did you have to ask?" Roberto asked. He sounded exhausted.

"Hey, I just wanted to have a family chat," I said with a shrug. "You know, do some bonding? I thought that was why I was sent here to live with the guy who abandoned me."

Roberto sighed, and I could tell Lauren was on the verge of saying something that would definitely annoy me—like reminding me that coming to London had been *my* idea in the first place. So I cut her off.

"I'm sorry if I said the wrong thing. I promise I'll keep my mouth shut in future family conversations that don't require my opinion."

I stood, gave an exaggerated curtsy, and went to my room.

Once inside, I hid under the warm comforter with my headphones on, listening to my Sad Songs playlist. I squeezed my eyes shut, trying to believe that when I opened them again, I'd be back at home, watching a telenovela with my mom while she stroked my hair.

I could almost smell the garlic on her hands after she'd spent the whole day in the kitchen, preparing the frozen meals she sold for a living. I could almost see the reproach in her loving dark brown eyes, which seemed to say more than her words ever did. I could almost hear the lecture she would give me, her voice kind but firm: *Was this how I raised you, Dayana? To make a scene in someone else's house? To not face your problems with your head held high? To hide from the world and forget that you have a whole life ahead of you? I didn't raise my daughter to give up when the going gets tough.*

When the image became too real, I opened my eyes and found nothing but the darkness under the comforter. I blinked, a little dazed, tears welling up in my eyes. It was painful to see her face, even in my mind. It was painful just remembering her voice.

I wanted so badly for her to be with me.

But she wasn't.

And it was my fault.

My phone pinged, distracting me from the thoughts I'd tried to bury in the depths of my mind. I jumped, my hand flying so quickly for the phone that I got tangled in the comforter and almost fell off my bed.

I dried my tears with the back of my hand and unlocked the phone.

Diana's name danced before my eyes.

> Tudo bem?

> Sorry I didn't respond last night, I was working the late shift

> I was really tired when I got home

No worries! The late shift sounds exhausting

Can you work before you're 18 here?

You have such a baby face, I didn't think you were old enough

Haha I'm 16

It's the age you can get a National Insurance number

Are you thinking of working?

I hadn't thought about it, but now that you mention it . . .

Maybe I am?

It was like a light bulb went off in my head.

My agreement with my grandparents was that I would stay with Roberto until I finished high school. Then I could decide whether to leave or stay. But the truth was that I didn't have a home anymore, not in England or Brazil. It still really hurt that my grandparents hadn't fought for me, and on top of that, I felt too much guilt to go back. But at the same time, my dad . . . well, my dad had abandoned me and didn't seem too concerned about making up for it.

What would I do when I finished school? That was the question I'd asked myself most since deciding to move here.

And suddenly it was like I'd seen a light at the end of the tunnel. If I started working and saving money, I could support myself more quickly. I could live on my own without anyone getting in the way.

It was perfect.

Like a sign from my mom.

My phone pinged again.

Glad to be of service ☺

Do you need help? I can explain how things work here

And I might know of an open position . . .

I'll let you know

Seriously??? You must be an angel that fell from heaven

Or from the palace fence?

Fallen angel works for me ☺

Are you free today?

It's my day off

I can take you somewhere much better than that mixuruca palace

I couldn't help laughing—she'd used one of my favorite Portuguese words. Nothing in English could capture it, though the closest thing is probably *gaudy*.

I bit my lip, trying to contain my excitement, but it wasn't easy. My heart was racing as if I were still running through the streets of London with her, holding hands as we fled from an unknown danger.

I knew basically nothing about Diana, and this was only the second time we'd spoken, but talking with her made me feel alive. And I hadn't felt like this since my mom died.

Maybe that, combined with my curiosity about her, was why—after texting *What time?*—I went on a royal gossip site for the first time in ages and started catching up on the news.

If Diana really did have something to do with the royal family, then things were going to get interesting.

Trouble in Paradise?

Another source confirms Prince Arthur's affair

by Chloe Ward

As Shakespeare would say, there's something rotten in the state of Denmark—or, in this case, England. After rumours of infidelity (<u>read more</u>), another source has confirmed that the heir to the throne is having an affair. "On Saturday, Arthur and Tanya met at the palace to discuss a possible separation," the source told us.

Another witness revealed that the same woman caught with the prince at the Royal Ascot race was seen heading toward the Queen's office on Sunday.

Outside the palace walls, the public is dying to know: Will Arthur follow in his mother's footsteps and separate from the duchess?

Chapter 6

I met Diana at the Camden Town station.

Riding the London Underground wasn't exactly a breeze. For a born-and-bred Carioca like me, who was used to having only two subway lines that covered less than a third of Rio de Janeiro and ran parallel for a bunch of stops, keeping track of the ups and downs and transfers of "the Tube" was like taking a college entrance exam. Getting to Buckingham Palace the previous day had taken me twice as long as my phone said it would.

Thank god for Google Maps.

I was paying even more attention to the app than I had to Diana the day before, and that's saying something.

I spotted her near the turnstiles. In black sweatpants and a crop top, she looked a lot more comfortable than she'd been the day before, running from the palace. The smile that lit up her face when she saw me made my stomach flip.

No one should be allowed to be that beautiful.

"We didn't have much time to talk yesterday," she said as we started walking. She didn't mention the *reason* we didn't have much time—aka the palace guards chasing us. "Have you been in London long?"

She spoke Portuguese slowly, like someone learning a new language, but also in a really cute way.

"Three days," I replied.

Diana's eyes widened, and even I was surprised by how little time had passed. It felt like so much had happened.

"Are you here on vacation?"

"No, I moved here to live with my . . . dad." I hesitated, but since I still wasn't ready to talk about it, I added, "So, is this a *hot spot* for young people?" It sounded like something my mom would've said, and I stifled a giggle.

Diana wrinkled her brow, confused by the unfamiliar term.

"Is this where teenagers usually hang out?" I rephrased the question as we stopped at the entrance to Camden Market.

Earlier, I'd looked up the market online and learned that it was basically the English version of Saara, the famous spot in downtown Rio where hundreds of street vendors sold products of questionable quality for much lower than the market price.

Unlike Saara, though, Camden Market was surrounded by walls. Inside, there were a million little shops that sold all kinds of things: From clothes and souvenirs to paintings and mirrors and decorative plaques, you could find literally *anything.* My mom would've loved it. Every time we traveled, she made sure to buy souvenirs, even if we were only an hour from home. I'd brought her whole collection to London—it was one of her many belongings I couldn't manage to let go of. As I took in the sights of Camden, I realized that I had to buy something there. My mom might not be physically present, but she would always be with me, no matter where I went.

Before I could go wild at the little stalls, Diana led me down a passageway where an incredible mix of smells wafted toward us. Food smells.

My stomach growled—or sort of rumbled with happiness— and Diana smiled. I noticed for the first time that she had a slight overbite, and her two front teeth were bigger than the rest. She was smiling so wide I could see the dimple on her right cheek. Tiny freckles dotted her face, with some bigger ones sprinkled between her eyes and the tops of her cheeks. Four of them stood out above the groove of her upper lip, and for some reason they reminded me of the Southern Cross, a constellation I used to see back home.

As soon as I realized I was staring, I dropped my gaze. God, this was so embarrassing! She probably thought I was staring at her *mouth.*

Which, actually, I was.

But she didn't need to know that.

I waited a few seconds, hoping the uncomfortable moment

would pass, then looked up again. Instead of pretending nothing had happened, Diana was still standing there watching me, her eyebrows raised, her smile even wider than before. It was like she was *teasing* me.

Crap.

What did it mean? Did she *like* me? Or did she just think it was funny that I couldn't hide my crush on her even a little bit?

I looked straight ahead.

"Let's go?" I said in English, revealing my terrible accent and avoiding her gaze.

Diana nodded, looking almost smug. I had a sudden urge to punch her pretty face and take off running, but I just ignored her and kept walking.

She caught up to me and started pointing at the stalls, explaining what kind of food they sold.

"Indian. Japanese. Chinese. Taiwanese . . ."

I stopped in front of each one for a better look. I didn't even know where to begin. If there was anything I liked more than eating good food, it was trying something new. Sure, it could turn out to be awful, but I wasn't that picky. I usually liked almost everything I tried.

I finally chose a Thai stall and ordered a delicious (and very spicy!) shrimp pad thai, plus a pork skewer with peanut sauce, which I loved from the first bite. Diana got a vegetable yakisoba at the Japanese stall next door. She told me that Camden was one of her favorite places and she'd tried pretty much all the food there.

I felt a crazy urge to make it my favorite place, too. To share it with her.

We sat down in an area full of concrete picnic tables, talking about everything and nothing as we savored our meals. We chatted about music—she liked indie, grunge, and folk—and about our favorite things in England and Brazil without ever getting to anything important, like her escape from the palace or my move to London. I don't know if she thought my move was a sensitive subject, just the way I figured her secret was for her, but it was clear that we understood each other like no one else.

My eyes wandered over the people, the food stalls, the little shops in every corner, then back to the people from all different countries strolling through the open-air market. From time to time, I noticed Diana watching me, as if she wanted to know what I was thinking.

Could she really be as curious about me as I was about her? She must have wanted to know more about the girl who had so little sense of danger that she'd helped a fugitive escape from Buckingham Palace.

When we were done, Diana led me through more mazelike passageways into the heart of the market, past every possible kind of shop. I found a stall that sold hippie-type accessories and spent a while admiring necklaces and trying on rings. I left without buying anything—not because I have any self-control, unfortunately, but because I still had no idea what to do about money. Roberto and Lauren had decided to give me a monthly allowance of fifty pounds so I could go out and be at least a little bit independent. They also told me about an emergency credit card they kept in the top drawer of the TV stand. It was tempting to see the card dancing in front of me, begging me to take all the money Roberto hadn't sent my mom in the past ten years. But I had to be strategic. What if I did something stupid and Roberto decided to hide the card and cut off my allowance? Before I did anything reckless, I'd have to test the waters.

It was only when I stopped at the next stall that I decided to make my first purchase. The little souvenir shop was the cheapest I'd seen so far, and my eyes immediately landed on a snow globe—one of my mom's favorite kinds of decoration. It had a black base, and inside the glass was our beloved Buckingham Palace.

It was funny to think I'd met Diana at that very spot, and in the strangest way possible.

Out of the corner of my eye, I watched her examine a rack of key chains. Her red hair shone in the light reflected off the mirrored ceiling. When we left the shop, she took my hand firmly, as if to guide me somewhere. We passed a bunch of street artists and musicians, some of them playing music that made me bob my head, and finally ended up in a larger space full of dessert stalls and more picnic tables.

"Have a seat," she said, gesturing at an empty table. "I'll be right back."

And she walked off quickly. I watched her narrow shoulders until they vanished into the crowd.

The place wasn't packed, but it was pretty busy for a Monday. An endless stream of people flowed from the same passageway we'd come from. Some of them looked for open tables, while others went straight to the stalls, ate standing up, and then started walking again. A dark-skinned man with tattoos on his arms played a stylish black guitar that was covered in band stickers. He sang the final words of an Ed Sheeran song in a gravelly voice, then started on "Hero" by Family of the Year. Passersby tossed coins into his case and continued on their way when the song ended, and he thanked the small audience that had stuck around before launching into the first chords of a song I knew by heart. "Canyon Moon" by Harry Styles. I smiled and closed my eyes, relishing the moment, and bounced my leg to the rhythm as I sang along.

I didn't open my eyes until the song was almost over. I gazed at the talented musician, who sang with a charming smile on his face, and only then noticed Diana standing a few yards away from me, two little containers in her hands. She couldn't have been there long, but I was still dying of embarrassment. She gave me an adorable smile and held up the containers to show me what she'd bought: a cup of hot chocolate and an order of churros. My eyes lit up with excitement when she sat down beside me and offered me a churro. I took one, dipped it in chocolate, and took a bite.

"These are common in Brazil, né?"

The way she said *né* was so cute I wanted to pinch her cheeks.

"Yeah, but they usually have a filling. Most of the time it's doce de leite."

"Dulce de leche," she repeated, pronouncing it like a Spanish speaker. I laughed at her accent, and Diana grinned. "So . . . did you enjoy our adventure?"

"I loved it! Thanks so much for bringing me here. Really." I took another bite of churro and decided to make a confession. "My first days in London haven't been that great."

"Why not?" she asked, her eyes brimming with curiosity.

Maybe we were finally going to talk about the important things.

"I had to come because . . ." I looked away, hesitant. Why was it so hard to say it out loud? "My mom died. And I didn't have anyone to live with."

Which wasn't completely true.

"I'm so sorry."

Her face was full of sympathy.

I took a deep breath. "I don't get along that well with my dad, so it hasn't exactly been a walk in the park."

"Is that why you're looking for work?"

"Yeah. I think it would be good to have some savings. Nunca se sabe."

She frowned at the expression, and I searched for the translation in my head.

"You never know."

"This might seem weird, but I totally understand. I've had some problems at home, too—my mom and I have been fighting a lot. Working helps me relax." Diana bit into another churro, and a little chocolate smeared the corner of her mouth. "Anyway, if you came to live with your dad, he must have gotten you a Resident Permit. If you have a BRP, your National Insurance number will be on the back."

I must have looked bewildered by all the names and abbreviations. Diana laughed.

"It's a little confusing at first, but you'll get the hang of it."

"You said you might know of a job opening?"

"Yeah . . ." She pursed her lips, and I could tell there was some kind of problem. "But I'd have to introduce you to my mom."

"Oh!"

She gave a pained smile.

"And you're not in a good enough place to do that," I guessed.

Diana nodded. I had an urge to wipe the chocolate from the corner of her mouth, but I restrained myself and brought my fingers to my own lip instead.

"Does it have anything to do with what you were up to yesterday?"

Her smile was real this time, and a little crooked. I could see the dimple in her cheek now.

"Maybe."

I laughed at her evasive answer.

I hadn't learned anything from the royal gossip sites that morning, except a rumor about Prince Arthur's infidelity (shocking, I know!). Given that he was old enough to be Diana's father, I was *pretty* sure I could rule out that possibility. Even more so because I refused to believe the rumor was true in the first place. To me, Arthur and Tanya had always been a model couple. I admired the way they'd fought to modernize the royal family, often going against Arthur's grandfather, who was a classic rich old conservative. It was clearly an uphill battle to break with so many years of backward ideas—especially considering that the UK still had a monarchy well into the twenty-first century.

But besides that outrageous rumor, there wasn't anything new. Which meant that Diana's story was probably a lot less exciting than I imagined—she was probably the friend of the chauffeur of Arthur's fifth cousin, and he helped her sneak into the palace or something like that.

She ate the last piece of churro and wiped her mouth with a napkin before standing up.

"Shall we?" she said, as if trying to change the subject.

I studied the mischievous smile still playing around her lips, as if I could find the answer to my question there.

Finally, I gave up and rose from my seat.

I was okay with a few secrets as long as she didn't stop smiling at me like that.

"Emi," I blurted out when the music started playing over a montage of romantic scenes. "How did you know you were a lesbian?"

Emi looked at me from the other end of the L-shaped couch. Between us, Lara kept her eyes on the screen. Weekend movie nights were one of our traditions. That night we were at Lara's house, and the movie was Every Day.

"I don't know, amiga. I think I always knew? I used to pretend to kiss Lara all the time when we were younger, but she was never into it. A real tragedy."

Without turning her head, Lara stuck her tongue out at Emi. "I was just innocently trying to play house and Emi was over here trying to kiss me on the lips."

Emi rolled her eyes and gave Lara a little shove.

"But do you think you can realize it later on? Like Rhiannon?" I pointed at the main character on the screen. She falls in love with A, a person who wakes up with a different body—and therefore a different gender—every day.

"Definitely. We live in a heteronormative society, and I think it's normal for people to not figure out how they identify until later, or lie to themselves, or not recognize their own feelings. Especially if they're bi or pansexual. In that case it's probably a lot easier to think they're just confused."

"Hmm . . ."

A conversation started on-screen, and we fell silent. But I wasn't thinking about the movie anymore—I was turning Emi's words over and over in my head.

Chapter 7

The sound of the incoming video call filled the room. I stared at the photo of my grandma on the screen for a few seconds, trying to decide whether to pick up. A stab of guilt broke through the resentment I felt toward her and my grandpa, tempting me to answer. Logically, I knew they'd sent me to London with good intentions. My mom's death had been hard for all of us—my grandma was depressed for weeks and couldn't get out of bed even for meals. My grandpa and I had had to be strong so we could take care of her, even though we were hurting, too.

My mom had been gone for a month when my grandparents got a call from my school. They wanted to set up an emergency meeting to talk about my loss and how much it had affected my grades. It was on our way home from the meeting that it hit me: My grandparents were exhausted. Not just because of their daughter's death, but because now they had to take care of a teenager all over again.

So I suggested, "What if I went to live with my dad and finished high school in London?"

They looked at me, stunned, and I could tell the thought had never occurred to them.

"I mean, I know it's hard for you two, and it should be his job to take care of me . . ." My voice trailed off when I saw them exchange glances.

It was a spur-of-the-moment idea, and I regretted it as soon as I realized they were taking it seriously. They didn't even say, "Stop talking nonsense, Dayana, we're perfectly able to take care of you" before making their final decision. They just sat there in silence, thinking it over. Later, I overheard them make a call to Roberto.

It was painful to think that my grandparents hadn't made any effort to keep me. I'd just lost my mom, and all I wanted was to be with my real family, the people I loved. Instead, they'd abandoned me and sent me to live with a man who'd never wanted anything to do with me.

Maybe it was my punishment. Maybe my grandparents also blamed me for her death.

But still . . .

"Hi there, sweetie pie!" my grandma chirped as soon as I picked up.

I ventured a smile. It was one thing to pick a fight with Roberto, but I wasn't brave enough to try it with my grandparents.

"Hi, Grandma. How's it going?"

The screen showed only half her face, from the nose up.

I'd had to teach her how to make video calls about five times when I was still in Brazil because she kept forgetting. Sending WhatsApp messages was hard enough for her. On top of that, I'd had no desire to show my face, so we'd just had audio calls until now.

"We miss you so much, Day! But, otherwise, everything's good." She always said the same thing. I wondered if, deep down, she regretted their decision at all. I hoped so. "I've been missing your sweet little face, so I asked Neide's daughter to help me call."

Neide was our neighbor. Her twentysomething daughter, Cris, appeared on the screen behind my grandma.

"Hey, Day! How's everything in London? Really cold?"

"It's great, Cris," I lied. "It was pretty cold at first, but I think I'm getting used to it. It's almost summer here."

"Oh, right! Everything's reversed up there." She was wearing a navy-blue cardigan. "Winter came early here. The weather totally changed after you left."

"Rio is crying for me," I said, half joking.

Cris chuckled, and my grandma smiled.

"Rio isn't the same without you," Grandma agreed, her face wistful. "But I'm sure you're positively lighting up that gray old city."

"And how are you, Grandma? Taking good care of yourself?"

"I am, sweetie. No need to worry about me." She waved

her hand dismissively, forgetting that she was still holding the phone with that hand.

"I'll look after her, too, Day," Cris assured me.

"I just want you to focus on yourself," my grandma went on. "Be sure to learn as much as you can and try to get along with your father."

I almost laughed at that last one. What she was asking wasn't exactly easy.

"Of course, Grandma," I said vaguely, avoiding the subject. "And what about Grandpa? How's he doing?"

"He's good!" She turned her head, the camera just inches from her cheek, and shouted, "Hey, Tião! Come over here!" She smiled at me before turning the camera toward my grandpa. "Here, say hi to your granddaughter."

His face appeared on the screen. "Hello, buttercup," he said in his calm, quiet voice.

He was a man of few words, so after a short exchange, he shuffled slowly away. My grandma added some more words of encouragement before we hung up.

When the screen went dark, I threw myself on the bed in frustration.

It was the end of my first week in London, and honestly, the only good thing that had happened so far was meeting Diana. I hadn't seen her since our trip to Camden Market on Monday, but we'd been texting. Out of curiosity, I kept up with the tabloids, but none of them had said anything about a red-haired girl jumping over the palace fence. For now, the spotlight was still on Queen Diana and her first acts since taking the throne. The papers were talking non-stop about how she'd called for a review of the royal family's policy on diversity in terms of race, ethnicity, and sexual orientation. Despite all the drama when Prince Andrew came out of the closet, King Oliver had continued to ignore social justice issues. But Queen Diana had taken the opposite approach: She was starting to open the door. The royal family couldn't keep turning a blind eye to these debates, she said. It was high time for them to get involved.

The mood in the house still felt off, even though Roberto was doing his best to smooth things over with his laid-back attitude. Lauren and Georgia were immersed in a sort of cold war, constantly jabbing at each other and exchanging hostilities, but at least now my stepmom had stopped bugging me so much.

All this meant I'd spent the past four days holed up in my room, alone. School wouldn't start for another three months, but I'd taken advantage of my newfound free time to start improving my English. Besides watching movies and shows with English subtitles, I practiced with Diana.

I should've been happy to be left alone, but the truth was I felt lonelier and lonelier with every passing day.

I looked around the room, studying the bare walls and old furniture. Nothing about this house felt like a home. I knew

that without my mom, anywhere would feel cold and color-
less, but it was one hundred times worse in London.

After what felt like hours, someone knocked on the door. I
locked my phone, which paused the TikTok I was watching,
and sat up. I didn't want to give anyone the pleasure of seeing me miserable.

Georgia poked her head through the door.

"What is it?" I said coldly.

"Whoa, no need to be rude." She came in and shut the
door, then sighed. Her defensive posture relaxed. "I came to
apologize," she said simply. "I was a little upset the other
day, but I shouldn't have taken it out on you."

"Did Lauri—" I caught myself just in time. I'd almost used
Lauren's nickname in front of her own daughter! Even
though they were fighting, I didn't think Georgia would
have been very amused. "Did *Lauren* tell you to come talk
to me?"

Georgia raised her eyebrows. Had she noticed that I'd
stumbled over Lauren's name?

"No," she said firmly.

It seemed like she and her mom still weren't on speaking
terms.

"It was Roberto, then, wasn't it? I should have guessed."

I picked up my phone, making a show of ignoring her. I
didn't want her fake apologies. She'd made it pretty clear
what she thought of me the other day.

"He did come talk to me, but I was already planning to say sorry to you."

"Sure."

I kept a skeptical look on my face, but something sank in my chest when I heard Roberto had tried to make up with Georgia.

"Look, I'm not like that," she went on, more loudly now, as she came over and plucked the phone from my hand. I crossed my arms, ready to protest, but she didn't let me get a word in edgewise. "I don't have a temper, I don't yell at people, and I especially don't say anything that might hurt my parents. And it's not because I'm trying to be the perfect daughter. I respect my parents. We have a good relationship. Do they annoy me sometimes? Yes. Do we fight sometimes? Yes. Like any family, none of us is perfect." She gave a frustrated sigh. She wasn't looking at me anymore— she was staring at the floor, her brow wrinkled. "And this pain I've been feeling has put me in a really bad mood, especially when no one believes me. But I crossed the line—I realize that. It's true that I'm angry at them for not taking me seriously, but let's be honest: A lot of this stress actually has to do with you."

"Me?" I asked sarcastically, putting a hand over my heart in mock surprise. I knew I was being a jerk, but I couldn't resist.

She made a face, refusing to take the bait.

"Things have been different since we found out you were coming, okay? And it hasn't been easy for me to share my parents with you. Or see you insulting the people I love." It couldn't have been easy for her to admit any of this, either, but Georgia went on, "Anyway, none of this makes what I said to you okay. I know you don't have the same relationship with them that I do, and I know you went through a lot back in Brazil, and I shouldn't have treated you like that. I'm really sorry, and I promise it won't happen again."

Georgia looked up at me, and I blinked, speechless.

It seemed like she was genuinely sorry. I was taken aback—I hadn't expected her to try to make amends for the other day. I knew how to handle arguments and insincerity, but this?

I looked down at my feet, nice and warm in a pair of *Beauty and the Beast* socks.

"Thanks . . ." I said cautiously. An uncomfortable silence settled around us. "Um . . . are you feeling better?"

"Yeah, I am."

Her face did look brighter and more alive than it had the past few days. Georgia was almost a foot taller than me, with broad shoulders, good posture, and a lot of curves. She wore her hair in a high-braided ponytail, and I had a sudden vision of her as the perfect daughter: smart, popular, everyone's friend. A straight-A student.

"But for real, are you sure you weren't just hungover?" I

cracked a smile, and she rolled her eyes. But it was my version of a peace offering, and she seemed to understand that. "I mean, I saw you come home late on Saturday. You don't need to lie to me."

"It's true, I went out. But I didn't drink that night. I just met up with some friends and vented a little about my hothead of a sister." She collapsed onto the bed beside me, clearly making herself comfortable, and grinned ironically. I rolled my eyes, but I wasn't exactly annoyed by what she'd said. After all, she wasn't lying to me. "It wasn't the first time I'd felt like that, but it's gotten worse over time."

"And you have no idea what's causing it?"

"The only thing I know is that one day I woke up with this crazy pain in my whole body and couldn't even get out of bed. They said it was probably because I exercised without stretching and it would pass quickly. But it didn't." She shrugged. "It got a little better, but it didn't go away. Sometimes it hurts so much I want to throw up. I've been to three different doctors, but the tests never show anything wrong, so they all say I must be exaggerating. Two of them said I just want attention. My mom believes me, I know that, but I think she gets frustrated sometimes. Like she did the other day."

I nodded, unsure of what to say.

"And with you being such a pain in the ass, the poor thing's probably had it up to here," she said, bringing her hand to her forehead.

I shot her a look and gave her a little kick. "Get out of here. I open up to you for one second and now you're insulting me left and right."

She laughed and got off the bed. "What can I say? The conversation was getting kinda boring without your usual sass." Georgia headed for the door, then turned around with her hand on the knob. "I like it better this way."

Then she winked, and I couldn't help but smile.

"Don't you think it's past time you met someone new, honey?" my grandma asked. We were at Sunday lunch, and my mom had just said she had no interest in dating. "It's not good for a woman to be alone."

My mom caught my eye and made a face that said, Here we go again. I stifled a giggle.

"You're right, Mom. My heart breaks every morning when I wake up and remember I'm alone."

My mom's cousins laughed, and Grandma frowned.

"Be serious, Patrícia. I haven't seen you with anyone since Roberto left."

"Just because you haven't seen me with anyone doesn't mean I haven't been with anyone." My mom raised her eyebrows suggestively, and her cousins choked back another fit of laughter.

"I'm not talking about the shenanigans you all get up to nowadays. I'm talking about a companion, someone who can help you raise Dayana, maybe give her a little brother or sister."

My mom almost spit out her beer. "Mom! Another child at my age? God help me."

Grandma ignored her. "I bet Day would love to have a little sibling, wouldn't you, Day?"

Everyone looked at me. I shrugged, feeling pressured.

"Uh, a sister would be cool, I guess. But only if she

was my age. I couldn't stand a baby crying all the time."

This time my grandma made a face. She clearly felt betrayed.

"Maybe we can get ahold of a time machine so I can give you a sister, Day."

"Mom, please. If we had a time machine, we'd have much better things to do than give you another headache to deal with. I'm more than enough."

The table burst into laughter, and even my grandma couldn't resist. My mom gave me a conspiratorial wink.

Chapter 8

Grocery store.

The Portuguese equivalent was *mercearia* or *mercadinho*.

It was a term I didn't use often, but I remembered it immediately as I stood in front of the store. It was a simple building with floor-to-ceiling windows at street level, through which I could see the small shop with its blue-and-white color scheme. It would have fit right into all the movies I loved that were set in the English countryside. The upper floors were made of white brick and dotted with tall windows, curtains concealing whatever was inside.

Earlier that day, Diana had texted me the address and asked me to meet her there. The store was on a little residential street in south London—which meant below the River Thames, I realized, studying Google Maps as I got off the Tube.

Diana had said she would finally introduce me to her mom, Rosane, which must have meant they'd made up, or at least called a truce. So I put on the most formal outfit I owned, though I thought it might still be too casual: a pair of mom jeans, a black half-sleeve blouse, and matching black combat boots. It hadn't even occurred to me when I was packing that I might have to go to a job interview. But the more I thought about it, the more it felt right. If I worked, I wouldn't need to depend so much on Roberto. I'd have more freedom, and a chance to get out of that house—and away from Lauren—sooner rather than later. It was perfect.

I cleared my throat and smoothed my shirt, switching into professional mode. I paused the One Direction playlist I'd had on the whole way to soothe my nerves, put my headphones in my bag, and went in. As soon as I crossed the threshold, I hesitated, looking around for Diana. Three women stood at the cash registers to my left, waiting for customers. To my right, a row of self-checkouts stretched to the other end of the room.

"Can I help you?" asked the closest cashier when she saw me standing there looking lost. Despite her tired face, her voice was kind.

"Hi," I said shyly, also in English. "I'm looking for Diana."

The woman's accent was so strong I didn't catch a single word of her response. But she pointed to a hallway on the right that led toward what looked like a back office, so I just thanked her and headed in that direction.

I was nervous. I'd never worked before—unless helping my mom make frozen meals counted as work—and even though Rosane was Brazilian, which made me feel a little better, I had no idea what kind of questions she would ask. What if I was a disaster? What if she wanted someone with more experience? Plus, as decent as my English was, I was having trouble understanding the English accent. And didn't working at a grocery store mean dealing directly with customers?

When I turned down the hallway, which was packed with small offices separated by flimsy partition walls, I bumped into someone, and in my rush to step back, I tripped over my own feet and started to fall. A hand grabbed my arm, saving me from a full-on wipeout, and when I looked up, I found myself face-to-face with Diana—and that amazing smile.

For a second, my eyes rested on the constellation of freckles above her lip. God, she was gorgeous . . .

And I'd just made a complete fool of myself.

I straightened up, my face burning.

"Olá. Uh, I mean, *hi*," I stuttered.

I clasped my hands behind my back, trying to seem confident. Her presence made me even more nervous, maybe because she had a magnetic beauty that made it impossible for me to look anywhere else.

"Olá," Diana replied in Portuguese, making me want to hug her. "Ready to meet my mom?"

"Now that you mention it, I feel like things are moving a little too quickly. We've only hung out once, you know . . ."

She laughed.

"Don't worry, I already have plans for our next *date*." She said that last word in English and winked at me.

My heart sped up. Did *date* mean what I thought it meant, or had I misunderstood? And why had she said that particular word in English?

I hadn't actually thought about where our relationship was going yet. I didn't have any experience flirting with girls, and I didn't know when I should ask, *So are you into girls, or are we just hanging out as friends?* I hadn't identified as bi for very long, and my past female love interests had only ever thought of me as a platonic friend. When Emi told me about her hookups with girls, everything had always seemed so easy. I thought everyone somehow just *knew*.

But that wasn't really how it worked.

"Come on," Diana said, pulling me from my reverie. I realized I'd fallen behind.

I put my doubts aside and ran to catch up with her. "Did you and your mom make up?" I asked, trying to break the awkward silence.

She gave a resigned half smile. "Not exactly, but . . . we're avoiding the topic for now."

I was seized with curiosity. Did the topic have anything to do with her escape from Buckingham Palace? Were they fighting because her mom had figured out what she'd been up to?

But another part of me was thrilled: Diana had tried to deal with this fight with her mom just so she could help me out. Happiness ballooned inside me, and I had to bite my lip to hold back a grin.

"Anyway, what matters today is you," she said, stopping in front of a beige door that looked like all the rest, except for a plaque that read MANAGER. *Gerente*, I translated to myself. "Good luck," she murmured in English before knocking.

"Come in," said a calm, confident voice. The door opened to reveal a desk piled with papers and a woman sitting behind it, her black hair pulled into a low bun. When she saw us, she took off her round glasses, stood up, and walked around the desk. She was tall and lean, with wide hips and a formal yet simple way of dressing—the kind of style that only looks good on some people.

"Mom, this is Dayana." Diana introduced me in English, gesturing toward me with her palm up, like a waiter. She was polite, but I could hear a certain distance in her voice. "Dayana, this is my mom, Rosane, the manager of Sugar's Grocery."

Rosane reached out a delicate, long-fingered hand for me to shake. I stood up straighter and grasped it firmly.

"Nice to meet you," I said, hating my accent.

When she smiled, her eyes crinkled so much they almost closed, and faint crow's feet appeared at the outer corners.

Rosane didn't look much like her daughter. Diana was a

little taller, with noticeably lighter skin and a more solid build. She had green eyes, while her mother observed me with dark brown irises. And Diana had a snub nose, the tip jutting out a little, whereas Rosane had a longer, straighter nose.

But their eyes had the same shape, tilting up at the edges so it looked like they were always wearing eyeliner. Both mother and daughter had straight, broad shoulders, which gave them naturally elegant posture. And that smile. Rosane's mild overbite and large front teeth looked just like Diana's, and the curve of their lips was almost identical. Her smile radiated the same sweetness and sincerity as her daughter's.

"You can call me Rose," she said in Portuguese, letting go of my hand and guiding me to the chair in front of her desk. "Diana told me you're Brazilian."

"I'll wait for you outside," Diana whispered behind me.

I looked over my shoulder in time to see her walk out the door, then sat down.

"It's a pleasure to meet another Brazilian here," Rose went on, settling into her seat. "I was born in Brazil, but I came to England when I was a little younger than you, so I don't know many Brazilians. Still, it's always so nice to run into fellow citizens, isn't it? There's something comforting about it."

"That's exactly how I felt when I realized Diana spoke

Portuguese," I said with a smile, remembering the rush of joy at hearing my native language in an unfamiliar city. "I've only been in London for a week, so I'm still trying to get used to it all."

"Diana said you came to live with your dad."

I shifted uncomfortably in my seat and nodded.

"Has he been here long?"

"Ten years."

"I see." She nodded and crossed her legs, putting an end to the subject. I could tell that the chitchat was over and the actual job interview was beginning. "How old are you, Dayana?"

"Seventeen."

"And why are you looking for work?"

I lowered my gaze and took a deep breath. Talking about my personal life was always a struggle, but if I wanted this job, I needed to show Rose that I was serious about it.

"I had to come live with my dad after my mom died." I felt a lump in my throat, but I forced myself to swallow it and keep going. "And school doesn't start until September. So I thought it would be nice to get a job that would help me practice English, and also save some money so I'm not such a burden on my dad."

It wouldn't look good to say I needed cash to escape from my stepmom as fast as possible, so I opted for part of the truth.

"I get that. It's one thing to depend on your parents when you all live together, but when you're on your own, it's different. I felt that way when I moved out of my parents' house. I always tried to avoid asking them for money. It didn't seem right somehow . . ."

Rose laughed, and I joined in. I liked her accent—there was something very British about it, but I also suspected, based on the singsong rhythm of her sentences, that she was originally from northeastern Brazil. She spoke slowly, as if she hadn't used Portuguese in a long time and was trying to get used to it again. But she still projected self-confidence. She had real physical presence without being loud; she showed strength without being harsh. And she knew how to hold your attention when she spoke: With her easy smile and gentle tone, she was like a mother talking to an obedient child. Lauren could probably learn a lot from her.

It was as if Rose's large eyes could see into my soul. Her tanned skin, a bit lighter than mine, seemed to glow. There was a sharpness, an elegance, to her face.

Finally, after what seemed like ages, she interlaced her fingers and put her hands in her lap.

"I don't know if Diana explained this, but our grocery clerk is about to start a summer class and won't be able to make the afternoon shift until September. It wouldn't be ideal to hire someone new for so few hours of work, which is why Diana thought you could replace Lily until she comes back. It's manual work. Pricing products, tracking inventory. We'll teach you how to use all the equipment, but the job also requires a good amount of concentration and physical agility. Workers under eighteen are paid £4.20 per hour. What do you think? Would you be interested?"

I blinked, overwhelmed by the barrage of information and the fact that . . . she was hiring me?

"Of course, it sounds great!" I was so excited that my voice came out abnormally high-pitched, but Rose didn't seem to mind. Quite the opposite.

"Are you surprised?" she asked, a note of amusement in her voice.

"A little," I admitted.

Rose chuckled. "I'm no stranger to the challenges of life in a foreign country. Even though I've been here for decades and have a UK passport, there weren't many people who were willing to give me a chance. And all because I was Brazilian. These days, I'm happy to be able to do that for fellow immigrants."

She smiled at me, her eyes brimming with empathy. I was dazzled—what an incredible woman Rose was. Like mother, like daughter, right?

She tapped her thigh, as if ending the conversation, and stood up. "What do you think about coming back on Monday morning to meet Lily, then? She'll be full-time for another week, but if you bring your documents, we can get the paperwork out of the way and she can start training you."

"That would be perfect!" I said enthusiastically, standing up, too.

Rose laughed.

"If you bring that attitude to your work, I'm sure you'll be an excellent grocery clerk. Lily had better watch out!" she said with a wink.

When we left the office, we found Diana sitting on a bench across from the door, staring at her phone. The smile that brightened her face was for me alone—she didn't even look at her mom as she fell into step beside us.

"I tried to convince Diana to work here, but she said it would be nepotism," Rose told me, laughing as she glanced at her daughter.

I didn't hear anger or pain in her voice. On the contrary, she sounded affectionate, the way moms do when they're trying to make up with their daughters.

Diana said nothing.

As we walked through the grocery aisles, Rose introduced me to a few staff members and told me her story. She'd been the manager for two years. She'd started out as a cleaner, and despite the barriers she'd faced as a foreigner, she'd proved to be a natural leader and had risen quickly through the ranks. Her story inspired me. I still didn't know what I wanted to do when I left school, but I'd have to start thinking about it soon. Learning that Rose had also faced moments of uncertainty made me believe I could find something I liked, too, even if it took a while.

Who knew—maybe Sugar's Grocery was the light at the end of the tunnel.

* * *

I was literally glowing with happiness when I left the store half an hour later, Diana by my side. A wave of heat washed over us, and the sun, which hadn't been out when I arrived, blazed overhead. I pushed my sleeves up as far as I could, feeling uncomfortably warm in my black top.

But not even the heat could put a damper on my excitement. I honestly couldn't believe I'd gotten a real job! I could have danced all night to the best song ever. Oh, oh, oh-oh. I could hear the chords of "Best Song Ever" in my head, my body begging to move to the rhythm.

"You look cheerful," Diana said, watching me with a little smile.

In the late afternoon light, her skin looked paler than usual, and her gleaming red hair danced in the breeze.

A gentle aroma of black licorice wafted over me.

We walked side by side down the street (I might have even been skipping a little). I had a new purpose in life, and I was determined to become a different person. I'd be fluent in English, I'd live up to my potential, I'd save money and . . .

Well, I didn't know what I'd do after that. For now, though, it was enough.

"I am. Really." I smiled back. "There's only one thing that could make me happier right now—a One Direction comeback."

"Ah, I see we have an overly optimistic Directioner on our hands."

I stuck out my tongue.

"Overly optimistic my ass. Mark my words: One Direction *will* be back."

Diana burst out laughing. I got the sense that a lot of my bad language went over her head, but that was part of why it was funny. So much of swearing comes down to the *feel* of it: You don't need to know the literal meaning if you get the tone.

"I guess I've been feeling kind of lost ever since I got here, you know?" I said more seriously, my hands in my pockets. "All this stuff with the move and coming to live with my dad after ten years and everything—it's really been getting to me."

I stopped abruptly, feeling like I'd said too much. I looked at Diana. She seemed a little confused, but also intrigued. I bit my lip and tucked a lock of hair behind my ear. It was weird how comfortable I felt with Diana, how I put my guard down completely when I was with her. Sometimes I had to stop myself from telling her everything.

"Speaking of being lost, where are we going?"

She pointed at a quaint little café on the corner.

"Didn't I tell you I had a plan?"

With a grin, she took my hand and led me inside. We picked a table by the front window.

"I wanted to show you a real London café. As opposed to a Starbucks full of tourists." She looked over the menu. "This place is one of my best finds. I come here so much that I've figured out all the cool combinations you can do, like . . ."

Now it was her turn to chatter away in her native language, and pretty soon she lost me in all the café's drink options. Instead of interrupting, though, I sat back and watched her. She was focused on the menu, her long, pale fingers riffling through the pages. There was a tattoo around her right wrist that looked like a band of interwoven flowers. My eyes rose to her face. Diana wasn't exactly my type: She was a bit too thin and white for my taste. But there was something about her . . . something that made her stand out. An undeniable charm.

Diana looked up at me suddenly and raised her eyebrows. I blushed as she handed over the menu. She'd caught me in the act again, just like she had in Camden Town.

"What do you think?" she asked. I squirmed, unsure of what to say.

"Pick whatever you think I'll like," I said, dodging the question.

Diana laughed, either because she realized I hadn't

listened to anything she'd said or because she just thought I was funny—I wasn't sure which.

She signaled to the waiter, a guy who was a little older than us and covered in tattoos, and put in our order while I sat there like an idiot. When two English people talked to each other, it was even harder for me to understand.

Once he'd left, she folded her hands on the table and leaned toward me. "Why were you looking at me like that?"

If we'd already had our drinks, I would have choked on mine.

"Like what?" I asked, trying to sound innocent.

"Like you want to dig up my darkest secrets?"

My jaw dropped. "What? I wasn't looking at you like that!"

Diana started cracking up. As she leaned back in her chair, still laughing, I tried to pull myself together.

Now that she mentioned it, maybe I was. A little.

"I was just curious." I decided to be honest. "The way we met wasn't exactly normal. There's a ton I don't know about you."

She looked at me thoughtfully.

"Maybe one day I'll tell you. Quem sabe? It would be a real vote of confidence. How do you say it in Portuguese again? You have to earn it?"

I bit my lip, suppressing a smile, and looked out the window at the quiet street.

"Thanks so much for your help today. Really." I turned

back to her and saw that her face had softened, though she was still studying me. "And thank your mom for me, too. Whenever you guys are talking again," I added, raising my eyebrows.

She let out a snort.

"You could tell, huh?" Her gaze lingered on my face. It seemed like she was trying to figure out whether I was trustworthy or not. She must have decided I was, because she went on, "We're having a bit of a . . . *disagreement.* I found out that she lied about something important, and I don't think I'm ready to forgive her yet."

Now she was the one who looked out the window, though I could still see the pain etched into her face. I felt a surge of gratitude that she'd confided in me, and I decided to do the same.

"I totally understand," I said, trying to comfort her. "My dad let me down, too. He abandoned me ten years ago. That's why this move has been so terrible. I had to come live with this guy who's basically a stranger to me after my . . ." I took a deep breath. Would talking about it always hurt this much? "After my mom died. He's a scumbag who never did anything for us, and suddenly everyone's acting like I'm the worst person in the world for not being happy about the chance to live in London and have a father. But I did just fine without him until now."

I realized my voice had gotten louder and louder, and I

paused to take another breath. The subject of Roberto always set me off.

"Family . . ." was all Diana said.

She knew there were no words to ease the pain we both felt.

We smiled at each other, full of comprehension. It was like we'd just shared a secret that only the two of us knew. Like we'd created another bond between us.

Right then, the waiter showed up with our drinks and a slice of cake on a tray. I admired the double-walled glass mugs, which had a rounded base but narrowed at the top. He put the first one—a pink, watery drink full of ice—in front of Diana. Mine looked like a green Frappuccino with a lot of whipped cream on top.

Diana thanked him but kept her eyes on me.

"Cheers," she said, raising her glass as if to toast.

I clinked my glass against hers.

"Cheers," I repeated, studying the word in my mouth. Diana nodded approvingly.

The drink tasted like matcha and sent a pleasant feeling through my body.

Or maybe it was just Diana's smile, which apparently had the power to mess with my nerve endings.

The scent of citrus hit me before I saw her. I looked up anxiously, just in time to glimpse Angélica passing my desk on her way to the back row.

My heart sped up. I had to stop myself from turning around and following her with my eyes.

The first semester of ninth grade was almost over, and though I'd known most of my classmates for years, Angélica was a new face. On the first day of class, she'd showed up in her school uniform shirt and a pair of jeans instead of the track pants the rest of us wore. She was a new student who didn't know anyone, but she'd walked into the room like she owned the place. Her confidence swept me off my feet.

At the beginning, though, I convinced myself that I just thought she was pretty. That was all. She was pretty. And stylish, and effortlessly charming. I just admired her. And might have been a little jealous?

But in the days that followed, I couldn't stop thinking about her.

It became an obsession. She was always on my mind, including when I woke up and before I went to sleep. I secretly scribbled her name in my notebooks. I sighed when I saw her in the school courtyard. I could recognize her smell before I even saw her.

By the time I realized it, it was much more than simple admiration.

Chapter 9

I wasn't totally sure how Lauren and Roberto would react to the idea of me having a job, so when I got home, I decided not to mention it. I'd have to tell them at some point, obviously, but I wasn't ready to risk ruining my happiness just yet.

Lauren and Georgia were in the kitchen baking something together. They leaned over a measuring cup, one of them holding the bottom and examining the markings as the other poured in wheat flour. Ruffles was curled up at their feet in a restorative sleep, letting out a little sigh every now and then. Once they'd measured the flour, they transferred it to a bowl and got started on the sugar. They exchanged enthusiastic smiles, like a mother and daughter in a margarine commercial. Ugh. They seemed to have made up.

I felt a twinge of jealousy. My mom and I were exactly the same: We cooked together a lot and loved trying new recipes, and we always had fun preparing meals to freeze for the week on Sunday nights. That said, it often annoyed me to have to spend part of my weekend working with her. Sometimes we'd argue, and she'd say I didn't have to help, that she could handle it on her own. Then I'd yell "Fine!" and stomp off to my bedroom, where I'd try to calm down by watching TV. When I started to get ready for bed and realized she was still down there, working herself to the bone, my anger would finally fade, and I'd shuffle downstairs to help her finish.

I'd thought we had so much time ahead of us, so many years of fighting and making up. Now I regretted not having been a better daughter.

I tried to sneak to my room unnoticed, but Lauren caught me.

"Hi, querida!" she greeted me, all smiles.

I'd always thought of Lauren as fake, but now I was starting to believe that her relentless positive attitude—even if it was kind of silly—was genuine. We jabbed at each other every chance we got, but she always greeted me with a cheerful smile the next day, as if she'd completely forgotten all our previous clashes.

"Georgia and I were just talking about the summer sale that's starting next week. You probably need to buy some new clothes, né? Moving to a new continent isn't good for anyone's wardrobe."

As Lauren chattered away, Georgia and I exchanged glances, trying not to laugh. She was well aware that her mom sometimes got carried away, and she shrugged at me as if to say, *But what can I do?*

I took a few steps toward the kitchen, trying to catch a glimpse of what they were making.

"At some point we'll sit down and figure out exactly what you need. That will help us decide which stores to go to. But Primark comes first, é claro! You're going to love it, it's simply enorme. But . . . hmm . . ." She looked me over as if measuring my body. I stiffened, feeling exposed. "I'm not sure they'll have anything your size. Maybe . . ."

Any good feelings I had about Lauren vanished in an instant, like a bubble bursting. My blood boiled. I didn't even let her finish—I just took a deep breath, trying to stop myself from causing another scene, then turned my back on her and left the room.

I was happy with my body. I mean, I'd be lying if I said I never felt insecure or unattractive for not lining up with society's beauty standards—I'd been on diets, I'd tried jogging around the neighborhood every day and not eating. But then it hit me that I was fighting who I really was; I was trying to change for other people, not for myself. I'd been fat since I was little, and it had never bothered me. But eventually, all the people around me saying I needed to lose weight, all the kids calling me a whale, all the adults telling my mom to stop feeding me junk food, all the times I cried in department store changing rooms because the clothes I liked didn't fit me—it all snowballed, and I started to believe there was something wrong with me.

When my mom realized how much the pressure to look like everyone else was affecting my self-esteem, she tried to comfort me by pointing out that I had a very balanced diet, and that the results of my blood tests mattered more than the numbers on a scale or the tags of my clothes. And that had been enough . . . for a while.

Until I realized that the people who had criticized me didn't give a damn about my health, which isn't relevant anyway. They were just trying to make me fit into an unrealistic standard— and I shouldn't have to fit into any standard to be respected.

What I ate or didn't eat was nobody's business. I didn't have to prove myself to anyone. My body was my temple; what mattered was that it existed and kept all my precious thoughts and memories. I just happened to be fat. Period. People just had to accept that.

Since then, I'd had my highs and lows, but whenever self-doubt knocked at the door, I made sure to send it packing.

That's why I didn't let anyone look at me the way Lauren had.

"Dayana? Amor, are you listening to me?" she called, but I shut the door to block out her voice.

Before I even reached the bed, the door opened again.

"Dayana, that was so rude! You don't turn your back on someone while they're talking to you!"

Lauriane looked like she was about to breathe fire. Small things could set her off, but she also didn't take shit from anyone. I shivered to think how alike we were.

"It was better to walk away than say what I was thinking," I shot back, but the floodgates had opened. "I feel good about my body, and I'm not going to put up with other people's criticism."

Lauren seemed exasperated.

"Dayana, I wasn't criticizing your body!" She sighed. "I'm sorry. I don't think there's anything wrong with your weight. You're linda in your own way. I just didn't want to bring you to a store where you'd feel uncomfortable because they didn't have anything in your size. I'm really sorry."

Whoops.

I blushed at the realization that I'd misjudged her.

"Look, querida." Her voice was calmer now, even kind. "We know you're going through um momento difícil. When my own mother passed away, God rest her soul, it was really hard. But this attitude of yours isn't going to help. There's no reason to lash out at everyone—we're all doing our best to help you feel comfortable and em casa. What I mean is that you don't need to be so defensive. Help me help you."

She reached out her hand as if offering me a chance.

I knew the only person I should take my anger out on was my dad. He was the one who'd abandoned us. He was the one who'd left with the promise that we'd join him when everything was ready, so we could all have "a better life" in Europe, and the one who'd ended up meeting Lauren, asking my mom for a divorce, and, at the end of the day, living his "better life" with another family. But it was hard enough to control the anger I felt all the time, let alone control *who* I took it out on.

Still, I knew I'd messed up. And badly.

Lauren really had been patient with me, and she'd been trying hard to make me feel at home. True, she wasn't always the easiest person to deal with, and sometimes I wanted to slap her across the face just so she'd shut up, but at least she *looked* at me. She saw the pain I was feeling.

That was much more than I could say about my dad.

I looked at my bedside table, which I'd decorated with part of my mom's souvenir collection. The Buckingham Palace snow globe sat beside a mini Christ the Redeemer and a tiny replica of the historic Tiradentes steam engine. I knew exactly what she'd say in this situation.

Swallow that pride, Dayana. It's always right to admit you were wrong.

She'd told me that so many times.

So I dropped my bag on the floor and walked sheepishly over to Lauren. I ignored her outstretched hand because . . . well, I didn't have to swallow *all* my pride. But Lauren smiled anyway, and we headed back to the kitchen together. She returned to the batter I guessed would become a cake, and I leaned on the doorframe, the way I used to do back home. I watched mother and daughter work together. It didn't look like there was any room for me.

But Georgia noticed me standing there and turned to me. "Could you grab another egg from the fridge, Day?" she asked, as if I hadn't just been super rude to her mom.

I rushed to the fridge, trying to make myself useful.

"Do you guys, uh . . ." I began awkwardly, handing her the egg. "Do you know any good plus-size stores around here? Not the kind that only sells grandma clothes."

"Oh!" Lauren snapped her fingers as if picking up an earlier train of thought. "I was going to suggest Asos Curve. I've heard really good things about it."

"Monki has some great stuff, too," Georgia said, popping a piece of the chocolate she was chopping into her mouth. "I have some of their clothes in size large—that would be G in Brazil—and the quality is really high."

They started strategizing: Was the best approach to stop at Primark to see if they had plus-size options? Take a look and then go to Monki either way? I listened and nodded, chiming in occasionally and jumping up to help whenever Lauren or Georgia needed anything.

The egg Georgia had asked for sat forgotten on the counter.

Later, my dad came downstairs and joined us on the sofa to watch a stupid movie on Netflix, and we all ate the carrot cake with chocolate frosting we'd made. It was the first quiet, pleasant night we'd had since I arrived in London.

And even if it was only for a few minutes, I managed to set my anger aside.

For those few minutes, I felt like I was part of the family.

Okay, so I was interested in a girl.

Physically interested.

Romantically interested.

Did that mean I was a lesbian?

But what about the boys I'd liked? Had that just been a phase? Or an interest based on what I thought my heteronormative society expected of me?

No, I didn't think so. I really had been interested in them.

I took a deep breath and grabbed my phone from the bedside table. I opened the browser and—just in case—turned on incognito mode.

I like boys and girls, *I typed into Google.*

I felt like an idiot, but I clicked on a few links, one after another, until I found a word that stopped me in my tracks.

Bisexual.

At that very moment, my bedroom door opened.

"Day, I'm about to get started on the meals," my mom said cheerfully, rubbing her hands together.

"Mom!" I yelled, so startled I dropped the phone. "Can you please knock?"

"Okay, okay! Sounds like someone is a little stressed." She raised her hands in surrender. "Do what you need to do—I can handle things on my own today."

She shut the door, leaving me frustrated and alone. I reached down for my phone and pulled the covers over my head.

But of course then I felt guilty and couldn't focus on what I was reading. I heaved a sigh, got out of bed, and made my way to the kitchen.

And anyway, if there was anything that could distract me from my anxieties right then, it would definitely be cooking with my mom. There was nothing in the world I loved more.

Chapter 10

Working as a grocery clerk wasn't as complicated as I'd thought. On Monday, when I arrived at the store for training, Lily showed me all the tools she used on the job: the barcode scanner that she used to track inventory, the price tag gun, and—one of the coolest things—a sort of electric staircase that lifted me up to the highest shelves at the push of a button. She also explained how to put in orders if we were running low on something, how to store certain special products, and how to use the system that determined which shelves needed to be restocked. None of it was that hard, and Lily was super helpful, demonstrating everything slowly to be sure I understood. But it was a lot of information, and I decided to come back a few more times that week for extra training.

Diana didn't stop by that day—she worked the afternoon shift at a café a few times a week—but she texted to wish me good luck. And when I got home, she sent another message asking how it had gone.

I'm a little freaked out about how much I have to learn, but it's ok

Everything will be fine haha

I'm sure you'll do great!

I recommended you because you seemed smart ☺

When I saved you from those palace guys, you mean?

Haha exactly

I couldn't resist the jab, but she just brushed it off. Would she ever trust me enough to tell me her secret? *Try to forget about it*, I told myself, though I was dying of curiosity.

After our coffee date on Saturday, we hadn't talked about going out again. Maybe it was my turn to take the lead? She was the one who'd suggested our first two hangouts.

Lying on my bed in my street clothes, I bit my lip.

When's your next day off?

This weekend

Anything you want to do?

All I could do was grin. I was giddy, buoyed up by that feeling you get when you connect on a deeper level with someone and realize they feel it, too. I did a little dance in bed and started typing my response: *Lol still working on it, but I'll think of something.*

Before I could hit send, Georgia burst into my room. I scrambled to hide the phone under my leg.

"Jesus, Georgia!" I brought a hand to my chest. "Couldn't you give me some privacy?"

"Privacy? Sorry, we don't have that here."

She snorted and threw herself onto the foot of the bed. Our relationship was built on insults and snarky comments, but in a good way. She raised her eyebrows.

"Why'd you hide your phone?" she asked.

I shifted instinctively, trying to block it from view. This clearly confirmed Georgia's suspicions.

She gave me a devilish little grin.

"Well, I was going to ask about all your mysterious disappearances, but now I have my answer. A crush."

I felt the blood rise to my cheeks.

"It's not a crush. I was just talking to a wor—" I stopped myself. I'd almost said *work friend,* but I still hadn't told anyone about my job. "Uh, girl . . . who I know."

Mentioning a girl in these situations usually shut people

up. Yes, it was a dirty trick, but it also wasn't my fault if they couldn't let go of their outdated heteronormative assumptions.

"A girl you know, huh?" She raised her eyebrows suggestively, and I could almost feel my shoulders slump with disappointment. I obviously hadn't fooled her.

On the other hand, it was good to know that Georgia was so open to the idea. I hadn't really stopped to think about my sexuality in this new environment, mostly because I had more pressing things to worry about, like a dad who'd neglected me and a fake-ass stepmother—though I was starting to think she wasn't so fake after all.

Somehow, though, knowing that Georgia accepted me made me smile.

"Is she English?"

I nodded, relaxing a little, and pulled the phone out from under my leg.

"And how's your English? Can you guys communicate okay?"

I made a face.

"I mean, my vocab is pretty good. I studied English, and I had to take the IELTS to get into high school here. But my accent is shit. And I learned American English, so I'm having trouble understanding the accent here." I clicked my tongue disapprovingly. "Lucky for me, her mom is Brazilian, so she speaks Portuguese. I'm kind of jealous. Even though she's not fluent, she's not embarrassed to speak it, or to mix in English words when she needs to."

"You don't know that, though. No one goes around telling you what they're insecure about."

I raised my eyebrows. I hadn't thought of that. "Good point . . ."

"But don't worry, I'll help you build up your confidence in no time. Rapidinho." She snapped her fingers. "Only English from now on."

"You've got to be kidding," I moaned in Portuguese. We were both laughing.

"English, please!"

"You're the worst." I stuck out my tongue.

"Okay, we'll start practicing this weekend, then." Georgia clapped her hands. "I'm summoning both of you to the Tabernacle on Saturday. Six o'clock sharp."

"What is that?"

"London's gaming mecca."

I frowned. Georgia sighed, as if she had no patience whatsoever for a novice like me, though I could see the amusement in her face.

"A really cool place with board games, snacks, and even some old arcade games. I usually go with my friends, and I wanted to invite you." She pointed at me like she was Uncle Sam.

"And who says I want to go?" I asked, just to keep up the habit.

Georgia rolled her eyes. "Don't you know what *summon* means?"

I gave her a little shove. She laughed, but I also saw her wince.

"Ow . . ." she murmured, massaging her arm.

My eyes widened. "Oh god, I'm so sorry!" There was a note of desperation in my voice. "I didn't know you were still in pain."

She grimaced. "It never really goes away, but sometimes it gets worse. Don't worry, though, I'm fine," she added, noticing my panicked expression. She stood up, laughing again. "Don't forget to invite your friend to come on Saturday. Or should I say *girlfriend*?"

Georgia blew me a kiss and left the room.

I bit my lip, staring down at the unsent message on my phone.

I erased it.

Have you ever been to the Tabernacle?

By the time I started high school, I no longer had a crush on Angélica. Between summer vacation, our new class schedules, and the fact that she was dating a sophomore boy, it just vanished, like in a magic trick.

And then came Heitor.

It was actually kind of a relief not to hide who I liked anymore. I wasn't the kind of person who usually lied to my friends, and I didn't have any reason to. They wouldn't judge me.

But still, part of me was afraid. What if Emi thought I was only identifying as bi so people would think I was cool? What if Lara thought it was just a phase? And even if they supported me and encouraged me to come out, what would I tell my mom?

I knew my fears were unreasonable. But I wasn't ready to fight for something I still didn't fully understand.

So I kept quiet.

Chapter 11

When I got back from the grocery store for the second time that week, I decided it was time to tell Lauren about my job. Up until then, I'd always said I was going sightseeing, so my stepmom hadn't asked many questions. She'd just given me all the usual reminders: Don't stay out too late, let us know if something comes up, be sure to answer your phone. But soon I wouldn't be able to hide the fact that I was going to the grocery store every day.

Besides, I didn't even *want* to hide it.

So while Lauren, Georgia, and I were setting the table for lunch, I told them the truth.

Their reactions weren't what I expected at all.

Georgia raised her eyebrows and said, "Wow, I didn't see that coming. I didn't think you were exactly the working type."

Lauren ignored her. "I think it's great!" she told me, placing a dish on the table. "Having a job will help you be more responsible and practice your inglês."

Was it just me, or was that a not-so-subtle hint that I was irresponsible?

"That's what I thought, too. About practicing my English," I added. Because I *was* responsible—very much so. "I was thinking of spending the money on a tutor who could help me with speaking and listening. I wouldn't want to start school without being able to understand any of my teachers."

"Nonsense," Lauren cut in. I was about to argue when she went on, "Let your father and me pay for the professor de inglês. It's a good idea, but you should keep your money. There are so many fun things you'll want to do here in Londres—especially shopping! In fact, this gives us another excuse to buy some new clothes!" She clapped her hands, clearly thrilled.

That night at dinner, she told Roberto about my new job and the idea of getting me an English tutor. He froze for a second, his fork halfway to his mouth, as he absorbed what she said about the two of them paying for it. Honestly, some things never change. I may have lived under his roof now, but Roberto was still as stingy as ever.

"Sure, sure," he agreed, after a discreet nudge from Lauren. "Don't worry about it. We'll take care of it."

"Thanks," I murmured, my mouth full of Lauren's delicious shepherd's pie.

She winked at me, and I felt a surge of gratitude.

A few minutes later, when my dad and I were washing and putting away the dishes, he finally congratulated me.

"You'll do great. There are a lot of opportunities here in London—you just have to know how to take advantage of them," he told me, rinsing off a plate and putting it on the dish rack. "Unlike me."

He didn't elaborate, but I knew what he meant: He spoke almost no English and didn't have a college degree. He'd become a citizen when he married Lauren, but he'd never managed to integrate into English society.

It was weird talking with him like that, as if we weren't two strangers who happened to live in the same house. I looked at our hands, his in a rubber glove and mine holding a dish towel, both resting on the kitchen counter. The light brown skin of his arm looked nearly identical to mine. Back in Brazil, my grandparents constantly told me how much I looked like Roberto. Physically, yes, but also when it came to our mannerisms, like the way we both slept with one leg bent. Looking at him now, I had to agree, but none of it mattered. Any closeness I felt to Roberto was eclipsed by the knowledge that I'd never had the chance to experience it as I was growing up.

Maybe I should pretend I was studying abroad in London and he was my host dad, trying to make me feel at home, but without any of the emotional responsibility of a real father. Believing in that version of things would be much less painful.

I watched him scrub the dishes, his big, friendly brown eyes exact copies of mine, and wondered if one day I'd manage to ask him the questions that really mattered.

* * *

I may not have been able to ask the important questions, but I was finally ready to squeeze out of Roberto all the money he owed me from the past ten years. And so, the next Saturday, when we discovered that Primark actually did have a plus-size section, I banished every last shred of guilt—and all my mom's advice about making pragmatic clothing choices—with a malicious grin.

I was ready to go wild!

But of course Lauren was there to rein me in.

"Okay, meninas, we'll meet back up at the cash registers," she told us, immediately taking charge. I'd almost forgotten that she handled the money in this family. After all, hadn't she been the one whispering on the other end of the line whenever I asked Roberto for financial support? "You can pick whatever you want—within reason. We wouldn't want to bankrupt your pai now, would we?

Maybe I would . . .

"And, for obvious reasons, Day has a higher spending limit," she went on. Georgia wrinkled her nose. "But still, let's control ourselves. Primark isn't going anywhere. Priorities, am I right, querida?"

I nodded, obedient as a dog. I'd just been bribed and manipulated, but I didn't care.

I looked at Roberto and noticed that he seemed just as excited as I was. He'd spent our whole drive to the store gushing about London, as if he was anxious for me to like it, which actually would have been kind of sweet, if not for that little detail of him having abandoned me when I was six years old.

When Lauren sent us off on our own, I started from the beginning. I took a quick look at every rack to get an overall sense of things, then headed to the fitting room with some jeans and a few tops to figure out what my Primark size was. The numbers they used were completely different from the ones back home.

After I put on the first pair of pants, my phone started ringing. It was a video call from my grandma. She was finally getting the hang of it.

Or not.

When I picked up, all I could see was her ear and a few strands of graying hair.

"Grandma? Where are you?" I asked, amused.

"Day?" She was basically shouting. "I'm here! Can you hear me?"

She moved the phone away from her ear and looked at the screen. When she saw me, a smile lit up her face.

"Hi, sweetie!" Her eyes were shining. It was like she hadn't seen me in ages, even though our last call had been about twelve hours earlier. She brought the phone closer to her face, and I couldn't see her smile anymore, just her eyes and nose. "How's my beautiful granddaughter?"

"Your beautiful granddaughter is happily trying on clothes right now." I turned the camera toward the items I'd piled on the fitting room bench. "Your granddaughter is *very happy*." I said the last two words in English.

"Oh, I'm glad, Day!" Her eyes were brimming with pleasure. "It's so good to see you smile. So everything is going well there, right?"

"I mean, everything is still kind of strange, but . . . yeah, I think it's going well."

"You only arrived a few days ago. I'm sure things will keep getting better and better. You all just have to get used to each other, to being a family." She seemed to be saying this to convince herself rather than me. "I'm really proud of you, Day. It brings me peace to know that you're doing well. I could tell that, deep down, you weren't happy with the decision your grandfather and I made, but I hope you know we had your best interests at heart."

I was taken aback. This was the first time my grandmother had acknowledged that she knew how I felt.

There was a bitter taste in my mouth.

"I know . . ." was all I said. My good mood had completely vanished. "Grandma, you're breaking up a little. I'm going to hang up, okay? Love you."

Before she could respond, I pressed the red button.

I stared at myself in the mirror for a few seconds, until the fitting room curtain opened partway.

I jumped, trying to cover myself even though I was fully dressed. Then I realized the smiling face peeking in at me was Georgia's. The rest of her body was hidden behind the curtain.

"Georgia, you scared the hell out of me," I scolded her, though I felt much more relaxed knowing it was her and not some stranger.

She ignored me. "So have you figured out your size? Do you like the fit?"

I looked down at my legs and did a little dance. "Not too bad!"

Georgia rolled her eyes. "Sounds like you don't need my input."

She opened the curtain all the way to reveal a yellow gingham dress that hugged her many curves. "What do you think?" she asked, twirling in place.

"Beautiful!" I said, and I meant it. "Where did you find it? Do you think they have it in my size?"

"Oh no. You want to buy matching clothes now? People will start thinking we're twins."

"You know where you can shove that dress of yours?" I shot back, though I wasn't really annoyed. "I don't know, I just thought it might look good on me . . ."

Georgia snorted. "I get it. You want to look good for your girl."

When I started to protest, she cut me off.

"Okay, okay. I'll let you have it so you can impress your crush today. Give me a sec, I'll go get your size."

And she left before I could say another word.

It was definitely the happiest day of my life.

Emi, Lara, and I were glued to the car window as we pulled up to a gorgeous country hotel surrounded by greenery and wildlife. You could hear the birds chirping in the trees, and there was a huge pool you could see all the way from the parking lot.

My mom didn't have the money to throw the kind of fancy birthday parties I'd sometimes wanted. The previous year, I'd gotten obsessed with Hilary Duff after seeing A Cinderella Story and wanted to have a costume ball just like hers for my fifteenth birthday, with a princess gown and everything. All I got was a sky-blue cake and masks to hand out to my mere ten guests.

So by the time my sixteenth birthday rolled around, I wasn't expecting anything special. I'd learned from my past disappointments, and I was stronger because of it.

Which was why, when I woke up that May 29 to my two best friends jumping on my bed and telling me to pack my bags because we were hitting the road, I thought they were messing with me.

I'd never imagined that my mom would plan a whole weekend for me!

When I looked at her, grinning from ear to ear, she gave me a little wink.

"How do you like your surprise, Lady Day?"

If she hadn't been driving, I would have jumped on her and given her a giant bear hug. But it didn't matter—I had all the time in the world.

"I love it! You're the best, Mom."

Chapter 12

I jabbed furiously at the buttons, as if I could take out all my rage on the muscular character I was fighting. The sound of the arcade machines around me blended with the clamor of teenagers eating, talking, and laughing at full volume.

The Tabernacle really was cool. As Georgia had said, it was a cross between a diner and an arcade, with a bunch of pinball and video game machines and a closet full of board games. Georgia's friends were already there when we arrived: a girl with thick black hair named Kate Ward, whose accent was so strong that at a certain point I gave up trying to understand her; and Carter and Duncan, a couple who looked so much alike (short hair, patchy beards, and light skin of almost exactly the same color) that I thought they were brothers until they kissed each other on the mouth.

We talked for a while, and then I ordered a delicious milkshake while we played Azul, a board game whose pieces look porcelain tiles. But when the game was over and my glass was empty, the inevitable weight of disappointment settled on my shoulders.

Diana wasn't going to show up.

We'd been at the Tabernacle for over an hour, and I hadn't heard from her at all—not even a text. Georgia and her friends tried to cheer me up, but I was devastated.

I'd gotten all dressed up for her, with my new gingham dress and everything.

I couldn't believe she'd stood me up.

Since I didn't want to cry in front of Georgia's friends, I decided to hide among the arcade machines.

It was the tap-tap-tap of my fingers on the buttons that finally broke through my mental fog, clearing my mind of negative thoughts. Why was I so angry? I mean, I barely knew the girl. All I could say about her was that she'd fled from Buckingham Palace and her mom was Brazilian.

The escape from the palace . . . now that I thought about it, it was pretty weird, wasn't it? I could imagine my grandparents exchanging glances and shaking their heads: *That girl is probably mixed up with drugs.*

I was so focused on the game, I didn't even notice when someone came up beside me—until they bumped into my thigh. Startled, I let go of the lever and turned toward them, shouting, "What?"

Diana's face was just inches from mine.

"You lose," announced the machine.

My arms went limp.

Diana took a step back, her auburn hair swaying.

When our eyes met, she smiled, revealing her slight overbite and the dimple in her cheek. The constellation of freckles above her lip caught my eye, and for a disorienting moment, it was all I could see.

"Sorry," she said sheepishly.

I wasn't sure if she was apologizing for making me lose the game or for being late. I cleared my throat and adjusted my dress, trying to compose myself.

"It's okay, I was going to lose anyway" was all I said. An awkward silence fell between us.

That was when I noticed how flustered she was. She was panting, her forehead glistened with sweat, and her hair and clothes were disheveled.

Sensing my gaze, she smoothed her wrinkled skirt.

"Sorry," she said again, and this time I could tell it was for being late. "Something came up and I wasn't able to text you. I got here as fast as I could." This all came out in a burst of such thickly accented English that it took me a second to understand. She cracked her knuckles nervously.

"Is everything okay?" I asked.

Diana nodded. "I just need a minute to get myself together."

I took her hand and led her toward the exit, my brows knitted. When we passed Georgia's table, I mouthed, *Be right back.*

She gave me a thumbs-up. When Duncan and Carter realized I was holding Diana's hand, they grinned and whistled at us. I picked up the pace, dying of embarrassment.

The wind whipped my face as soon as we stepped outside. It was still light—we were nearing the summer solstice—but heavy clouds had begun to blanket the sky.

Except for a few people right outside the Tabernacle, the street was deserted. Diana and I walked aimlessly down the sidewalk.

We were still holding hands.

She looked at me. "You're really pretty."

I looked down at my dress, feeling my face heat up.

"Do you know where we are?" she asked as we wandered the streets of a quiet neighborhood of row houses. It did feel oddly familiar. I frowned. "It's Notting Hill," she went on. "Didn't you say it was your mom's *filme preferido*?"

I nodded, my eyes wide. I studied the buildings around us with renewed attention, as if to absorb every little detail.

Then I closed my eyes, feeling the wind run through my hair. She used to laugh so much when we watched that movie—I could almost hear her. *I'm also just a girl, standing in front of a boy, asking him to love her.* She would say those lines along with Julia Roberts every time, and she'd shriek with joy, like she was a teenager again, when Hugh Grant showed up at the press conference at the end.

Grief hit me like a punch to the gut.

All I wanted was to be with her again.

Noticing my silence, Diana asked, "What are you thinking about?"

I smiled sadly. "My mom."

I wasn't sure I could explain everything that was going through my head. The pain of having to leave the place where we'd created so many memories together. The guilt over what I'd done.

How much I missed her.

I looked around at all the charming, colorful little houses.

"We always dreamed of coming here together. She loved London. We used to watch English movies together, and she was obsessed with British bands—she went to all their concerts in Rio. We loved talking about what we'd do when we came here." I was rambling, my thoughts turning effortlessly into words, but I barely noticed. When I turned toward Diana, I saw she was watching me closely. "And in the end, I really did come. But not with her." *And it's my fault.* The words echoed deafeningly in my head.

Sometimes I imagined locking my memories of her in a big wooden chest and hiding it in a closet somewhere. Now I wondered if I'd run out of space. How many more thoughts could I fit in there in hopes of forgetting them, of not having to feel anything? How many could I stuff inside before the lid popped open and everything came pouring out?

I was starting to feel like maybe I'd hit capacity.

Diana had been studying my face this whole time, and now she gently took hold of my chin, forcing me to look at her.

"I know it's hard, but you have to keep going. She wouldn't want you to be unhappy."

I laughed weakly, slamming the chest shut. "That's for sure. If she saw me like this, she'd be all over me. I can almost hear her: 'Come on, Dayana, wipe that pout off your face. See the sights, go to the little cafés you always liked, and don't forget to stalk those One Direction boys.'"

Diana giggled. "Oh, right! I forgot you're a Directioner. Too bad you got here so long after they broke up."

I glared at her. "That joke's getting really old. How many times do I have to tell you they're on *hiatus*?"

Diana pressed her lips together, fighting back a smile. "For more than five years?"

"It's just taking a little longer than expected because of their personal projects."

"There's no way you're that naive, Day. The sooner you accept it, the better."

"Shhh!" I hissed, making her snort with laughter.

The sound softened me.

I definitely had my doubts about One Direction getting back together, especially since the boys' solo careers were going so well. But there was still a thread of hope I couldn't let go of, a desire to see them together again even if it was only for a one-time reunion.

I turned my attention back to our surroundings, taking in the details. The architecture of the houses. The colorful doors. The light emanating from the windows. The sound of silverware on plates, families talking together over dinner. It was perfect. Whenever I'd imagined myself living in England, it was in a neighborhood like this, in one of these little houses. Strange to think that not too long ago I'd dreamed of living in the UK, and now that I was here, all I wanted to do was leave.

Well . . . maybe not anymore.

But I still wasn't sure if I belonged here.

"Ain't no sunshine when she's gone," I sang suddenly, moving my hand to the rhythm of *Notting Hill*'s theme song. "Na na na when she's away . . ."

Diana cracked up at my improvised lyrics and then joined in, helping me with the parts I didn't know. Seeing her laugh like this—and laughing *with* her—filled me with a goofy, light-headed happiness. There was something going on in her life, too, though exactly what was still a mystery. I wanted to ask, so I could comfort her the same way she'd comforted me, but I wasn't brave enough to stick my nose into her life. I was sure she would tell me when she was ready. For now, it felt good to know I was helping in some way, even if it was just by distracting her for a while.

We kept singing as we walked arm in arm down the street, nearly shouting when we got to the chorus. Someone poked their head out a window and told us to quiet down, but we ignored them. A raindrop landed smack on my nose. I looked at Diana. She'd noticed it, too, because she took my hand right as a few more drops spattered down on us.

We ran like crazy, the rain falling harder and harder, until we found an awning to shelter under. When we finally stopped, we both bent over, laughing and trying to catch our breath at the same time. I glanced at her out of the corner of my eye, my heart thumping wildly from the run.

As our laughter died away, I straightened up, and Diana did the same.

But she didn't let go of my hand.

I looked at her, water dripping from her hair, and tried to read her thoughts. Maybe because I was caught up in the magic of the moment, or in Diana's sweet smile . . .

I leaned forward and kissed her.

At first it was only a peck. The slightest touch of my lips on hers. I wasn't trying to *kiss* kiss her. I just needed to express my happiness somehow.

But then she kissed me back. She didn't stand there stiffly, waiting for it to end, for me to realize what a terrible mistake I'd made—which part of me had imagined would happen. Instead, she brought her hands to my waist and pressed her lips against mine. When I drew back a little—just enough to see her freckles and the glint of her green irises—she gave me a mischievous grin that sent me over the edge.

So I kissed her again. For real this time.

My hand cradled the back of her neck, a few wisps of hair brushing my fingertips. Her lips were cold and a little salty from the rain. I sucked on her lower lip, the taste spreading into my mouth, and she brought her hand to my face, stroking my cheek. The way she threaded her fingers through my hair gave me chills. When her tongue touched mine, I shivered and pressed her up against the wall, completely lost in the moment.

Kissing Diana was everything I'd hoped it would be. And, at the same time, it was new, amazing, unexplainable. A kiss I'd never believed could really exist.

It was surprising, just like her.

Maybe I wasn't sure if I wanted to keep living in London. But I was one hundred percent sure that I wanted to live in that kiss forever.

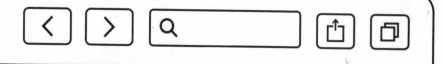

Mystery Teen Prowls the Palace

by Chloe Ward

June is shaping up to be a busy month for our darling royals. An employee at a convenience store near Buckingham Palace claims to have seen a certain teenager lurking in the vicinity in recent days.

"On Sunday, when I was finishing my shift, I heard shouting. Then two girls ran by, followed by security guards in dark suits," the employee reported. "But it happened so fast, all I saw was that one of the girls was a redhead." This description matches that of a young woman who, according to several eyewitnesses, visited the palace last Saturday.

The plot of this real-life telenovela is more intriguing by the day. We still don't know the identity of Prince Arthur's mysterious new love interest, and we can't help but wonder: What is his relationship to the teen delinquent giving palace security guards a run for their money?

Chapter 13

I was on cloud nine.

Every time I closed my eyes, I thought of our kiss. Every time I took a breath, I thought of Diana. Her voice. Her green eyes. The constellation of freckles above her lip.

It was Sunday, which meant I could sleep in. But I'd actually woken up early and spent a long time lying in bed, going over the events of the previous night more times than was probably healthy.

When I started to hear noise from the kitchen, I got up, practically jumping for joy, and went to help Lauren make breakfast. I must have had a ridiculous smile on my face, because she said, "Looks like someone woke up on the right side of the bed."

I grinned, unable to contain myself.

"Mmm, this is delicious," I said, nibbling on one of the pancakes she'd made.

Lauren raised her eyebrows, surprised by the compliment. Which, of course, was the perfect segue into her usual stream of chatter. I was almost used to it by now.

"Do you follow the royals, querida?" she asked suddenly. "Georgia and I are obsessed with them. It's all so fascinante!" She took another pancake. "We went to see Prince Arthur and Tanya Parekh's royal wedding and it was simply breathtaking. Maravilhoso! We *must* take you to the next royal event. You'll love it!"

Lauren launched into more stories about the royal family while I sweetened my coffee and continued enjoying my pancake.

"We went to see Queen Diana's coronation, too! And we even joined King Oliver's funeral procession, may he rest in peace," she went on. It was funny how Lauren didn't need any encouragement at all to keep talking. "Claro, we didn't get to see anything up close, but it was still very exciting. The whole family is so lovely, and I'm thrilled that Diana and her sons have broken with some of the royal traditions. A divorced queen! A gay crown prince! The younger son married to a foreigner! But all these rumors about Arthur and Tanya separating . . . we're heartbroken."

I froze with my fork in the air.

"But is it really true?" I couldn't help asking. "I thought it was just gossip."

"I did, too, at first. But Chloe Ward, who stalks the royal family for a living, is always the first to break big stories, and she's been dropping hints about this one for a while. Maybe it's nothing. It pains me to believe it." She shook her head as if Arthur and Tanya were members of her own family. "But other tabloids have started paying attention também. At this point, I think it's a ticking time bomb."

My jaw dropped. "Holy shit."

Lauren frowned at my bad language. The only thing that saved me from a scolding was Roberto's arrival in the kitchen.

"Good morning," he said, smiling at us and pulling out a chair. "Ready for our outing today?"

I blinked at him, totally lost.

"Actually, amor," Lauren said, putting a hand on his shoulder, "I didn't even mention it to Dayana because Georgia isn't feeling well this morning." She turned to me. "Your father and I were thinking of taking you two sightseeing today, but Georgia can hardly get out of bed."

My brow wrinkled with concern. Georgia had seemed perfectly fine the night before ... she wouldn't stop bugging me on our way back from the Tabernacle, so I finally gave in and told her what had happened with Diana. If I hadn't put my foot down, she would have kept me up all night with questions about every little detail.

"What's wrong with her?" I asked, forgetting the kiss, the possible separation of my favorite couple, and everything else.

Lauren tried to downplay the issue with a dismissive wave of her hand.

"It's nothing serious—not like the last time. But we thought it would be best for her to stay home and rest." Then her face lit up and she clapped a hand on Roberto's shoulder. He winced. "I know, querido! Why don't you and Dayana go on your own? I can stay here with Georgia." She might have been excited, but I could feel my own good mood sour. "It will be nice for you to have some quality time together, pai e filha. You've barely had a chance to talk since Day got here."

Any affection I felt for Lauren went down the drain that very second. I wanted to strangle her. But Roberto seemed to think it was a great idea.

"Of course! It'll be fun. What do you think, Dayana?"

I forced a smile.

What else could I have done?

* * *

An hour later, I found myself sitting beside Roberto on a classic red double-decker bus. Taking public transportation would save us money on gas and parking, he told me, but he also wanted to leave the car with Lauren in case Georgia had to go to the hospital. Apparently, Lauren didn't like driving, but she had a license and could use the car in an emergency.

Roberto also explained that they'd bought the car recently, after years of driving around in an old junker. It was hard to save money early on, he said, especially with the lingering effects of the recession, but little by little they'd set aside enough to pay off the house and then buy a new car.

Roberto told me a lot of things I had no interest in hearing. He seemed to want to justify himself for not having supported me and my mom. What he didn't understand, though, was that it was about more than just the money.

While he went on with his word vomit, I pulled out my phone.

SOS

Save me

Diana replied in less than five minutes.

Is it that bad being alone with your dad?

It's not bad

It's the worst

Despite what I'd said, I glanced at Roberto out of the corner of my eye, afraid he might be reading my texts. But he was still rambling on about the time their old car broke down in the middle of nowhere and he didn't have a bus pass or enough money to buy one, so he had to walk two hours to get home.

I angled my phone away from him when I saw that Diana was typing.

Lol

As much as I understand your resistance

I don't think it's worth it

You can try to live with your anger and not deal with it, but that won't do either of you any good

Or you can give him a chance

Hmmm

Can we go back to that part where we kiss

Instead of talking about things I don't want to hear?

You're so stubborn!

I'm all for the kissing part

But I'll still tell you things you don't want to hear

I suppressed a smile. The urge to jump up and run to wherever Diana was and kiss her again was waging a fierce battle against my better judgment. I took a few deep breaths.

Before I could text back, I realized Roberto had fallen silent. I looked up, worried he might have seen what I'd written, but he was staring out at the street. Was his monologue finally over?

Sensing my gaze, he turned to me with an awkward smile.

"Sorry to go on and on like that—sometimes I talk too much. Georgia always complains about it."

Of course she does. She's like a daughter to you.

I was surprised by my own bitterness. I wasn't mad at Georgia anymore, but I was still jealous that she'd had the chance to be a daughter to Roberto. And as my relationship with her grew closer, I only felt angrier at my father for depriving me of that chance.

It wasn't just that he'd left and started a new family, it was that he'd straight-up *disappeared*. He hadn't been the dad I needed, and he'd never even given me the opportunity to be part of his new family.

I didn't know what to say, so I just shrugged.

Unlike Lauren, who was kind of oblivious, Roberto said nothing, respecting my desire to sit there in silence. But he looked out the bus window with such a forlorn expression that I ended up feeling bad for him.

Ugh. I don't need this.

The thrill of talking to Diana was long gone, so I put my phone in my pocket and slumped down in my seat. As I watched the streets glide by, though, I started to relax. Taking the Tube was faster and more practical, but there was something magical about riding the bus, even when the heat was turned all the way up, filling the stuffy air with the stench of sweat. Sitting there on the upper level, like I'd always imagined, watching the old-fashioned London archi-tecture stream by—houses, shops, and businesses, all in that same classic, majestic style—sent a flutter of happiness through my body. I felt like Lily Allen in the "LDN" music video, seeing London through rose-colored glasses.

When we got off, I knew immediately where we were.

Behind me, Big Ben reached toward the sky, its hands marking three in the afternoon. Straight ahead, Westminster Bridge cut across the Thames in the direction of the London Eye.

Roberto led me toward the bridge.

"Where are we going?" I asked, finally breaking the silence.

"See that wall over there, in front of the Ferris wheel?" He pointed. "There's a path along the river there, and some good spots to just relax and enjoy the view. There are a few places to get snacks, too. I thought you might like it."

I was oddly moved by his thoughtfulness.

Once we'd crossed the bridge, we decided to grab a bite at

McDonald's. Roberto and I ordered the same thing: a McChicken, fries, and grape juice. I hadn't eaten at McDonald's in ages, but I couldn't resist. We took our paper bags and headed outside. The wall along the river was almost totally packed with groups of friends sipping beer and chatting, and we looked around for an empty spot to lean on while we waited for one of the wooden benches to open up.

From where we stood, we could see Parliament and Big Ben in all their pompous glory. To my right, an endless line snaked out from the London Eye. It was peak tourist season, and the whole area bustled with visitors and locals alike. The Ferris wheel was so tall, I had to lean my head all the way back to see the top. All its glass compartments were full. Roberto explained that he'd tried to buy tickets online, but they were sold out.

"I've actually never ridden it, but I'd love to," he said, taking a bite of his sandwich. "Apparently, sunset is the best time to go. Maybe it will be easier to get tickets in the fall." He took a swig of juice. "But don't worry, the view from down here leaves nothing to be desired."

He was right.

* * *

It was a sunny afternoon—London wasn't as gray as I'd expected, though it was constantly windy—and dazzling points of light sparkled on the dark waters of the Thames. Since the buildings along the river were all low to the ground, the clear blue sky felt endless, arching over our heads like the ceiling of a cathedral. Roberto offered to take a few pictures of me, and I posed awkwardly, the glittering London landscape behind me.

I sent the photos to Diana right away. It didn't take long for her to respond:

London's never looked so beautiful

I was walking on air.

When the sun started to set, tucking itself away behind the buildings, I leaned against the wall and admired the city. It was astonishingly beautiful.

For a fraction of a second, a terrifying thought took hold of me.

I felt at home.

Chapter 14

After the Sunday we spent together, I decided to give Roberto a break. The anger smoldering in my chest wasn't flaring up as often as before, and I thought I could give myself at least a week of peace.

Plus, my first official week at the grocery store was exhausting enough. The work itself was pretty mindless, but that didn't make it any easier. To avoid mistakes, I had to pay extra-close attention to everything I did, and I was probably a lot less efficient than Lily.

I knew this was normal for a new employee, and Lily herself told me not to be nervous and to remember that I was still learning. She also gave me her phone number in case I had any questions. Still, I was anxious. I wanted to do a good job. I wanted to prove myself.

By the end of the week, I was ready to collapse. My plan was to spend all of Saturday (and maybe Sunday) in bed, but on Friday night I got a text from Diana.

How's my little grocery clerk?

My. With a single word, she had my whole body tingling. *My.* God, I was pathetic.

> Exhausted

> Drained

> Destroyed

> Does that mean you're not up for hanging out tomorrow?

My body said *That's exactly right, I'm not getting out of bed all weekend.* But my fingers typed:

> For you, I'm up for anything

And so, early the next morning, I headed to the Tube station near Roberto's house to meet Diana. She was waiting by the turnstiles, and when our eyes met, she greeted me with one of her stunning smiles. Then she interlaced her fingers with mine, reducing me to a puddle on the floor.

"Bom dia," she said, guiding me into the station. "Looks like you had some trouble getting out of bed this morning."

"Can you tell?" I rested my head on her shoulder as we

rode down the escalator, closing my eyes for a second. "I'm worn out. Wake me up when we get there."

"Hey!" She patted my face lightly, pretending to slap me awake. "You said you were up for anything!"

I straightened up, giving her the biggest smile I could manage.

"I'm great. Not tired at all." Though my puffy face and droopy eyelids proved otherwise.

"We can postpone this if you want, it's no problem," she said sympathetically. But something in her tone put me on the alert. "Our trip to Princess Park Manor can definitely happen some other time."

My eyes bugged out. "What? Princess Park?!"

Diana bit her lip, holding back a grin.

Princess Park was where the members of One Direction lived when the band was first starting out.

"Mm-hmm. I thought you might want to see the place where your favorite heartthrobs used to live. Then I was going to take you to an ice cream shop called Milkshake City."

No *effing* way!

The ice cream shop One Direction used to go to? They even had a milkshake in honor of the band!

Diana finally had my full attention. I turned to face her, jumping up and down as we approached the end of the escalator.

"Oh my god, oh my god!" I squealed, making her burst out laughing. "I can't believe it!" I took her face in my hands and kissed her right there, in the middle of the Tube station. She swatted my hand gently, but she didn't seem annoyed. "My god, you're perfect!" I exclaimed.

"That's what they say," she said smugly.

I would have said something snarky if I hadn't been absolutely freaking out at the thought of visiting the most iconic place in One Direction's history.

I spent the whole ride telling Diana about my relationship to the band. We traded my headphones back and forth, listening to my playlist, and I explained how I'd discovered One Direction and what it felt like to see them live in Brazil. I was still a kid then, but luckily I had a mom who was obsessed with British music and understood how desperate I was to see my favorite band in person. She took Emilly, Lara, and me to their concert in Rio, at Parque dos Atletas. It was definitely one of the best days of my life.

My chest tightened when I pictured my two best friends. As Diana and I walked down Coppetts Road, admiring the houses along the way, I let myself think about them for the first time in ages. How were they? They'd lose their minds if they knew where I was.

"Why are you making that face?" Diana cocked her head, studying me.

Crazy how she could already sense changes in my mood.

I pulled myself back into the present, away from Emi and Lara, and smiled at her.

"I was wondering how much longer the hiatus will last."

Diana gave me a little shove, sending me staggering off to the side. We both laughed.

"Stop deluding yourself, Dayana!"

"Shouldn't you be supporting me and telling me to chase my dreams?" I asked in mock indignation.

"I'm more of a realist."

I rolled my eyes. "You're going to eat those words, just you wait."

Diana looked puzzled. "Is that a Brazilian expression?" she asked.

She was so cute when she tried to understand my Portuguese. Her brow wrinkled and she pouted a little, which accentuated the constellation above her lip. Her cheeks, flushed from our walk in the sun, almost begged me to caress their warm, freckled skin, to trace the tiny dots as if they formed a route on a secret map and . . .

Damn. I had it bad for this girl.

For all the little quirks that made her who she was.

Without a word, I took her face in my hands again, the way I'd done on the Tube. When our lips touched, she opened hers partway. Then she grabbed me by the waist and pulled me closer, and I ran my fingers over her sweaty skin and up into her reddish hair so eagerly that she laughed into my mouth.

She was stronger than me, I knew that for sure. If there was a storm raging inside me, then she was my lifeboat. And I was going to hold on to her with everything I had.

Chapter 15

The problem with relying on someone to be your lifeboat is that people are unpredictable. One minute they're taking you to an ice cream shop with a milkshake named after your favorite band, and the next they're ghosting you.

A few days after our trip to Princess Park, I'd lain on my bed and pulled up my text thread with Diana.

> **Just got off work**

> **What's up with you?**

I'd messaged her as soon as I left the grocery store, but she hadn't responded until hours later, after I'd finished dinner.

> **Exhausted and dying for a day off**

Of course—she'd been working. I remembered her saying it would be a busy week. That was why she was responding

less and less often and sending shorter and shorter
messages . . . right?

> Aren't you off tomorrow? Want to hang out?

> After the amazing day you planned for me,
> I've been wanting to do something for you

Diana's status indicated she was online, but it took her a
while to start typing. I had a sudden vision of her staring at
her phone, trying to come up with an excuse.

Finally, she wrote back:

Unfortunately

Não vai dar

I have plans tomorrow

> No worries, it can wait

> Maybe this weekend if that's better for you?

Things are actually pretty crazy for me right now

But let's keep talking, ok?

I frowned at the screen, feeling hurt, then turned off my phone without texting back. Was she blowing me off? After so many incredible dates? After that perfect Saturday at Princess Park?

Had she met someone else? Had she lost interest in me?

I turned facedown on the bed, devastated. I thought about putting on my favorite playlist, but then, to my horror, I realized I didn't want to listen to One Direction. It would remind me too much of Diana.

* * *

When I got to the grocery store the next day, I was even more of a mess. Diana hadn't sent any more texts, and I'd spent the whole night tossing and turning, wondering what had gone wrong. At one point, a terrible thought had occurred to me—*What if she's ashamed of me?*—and after that I really couldn't sleep. I didn't want to believe that Diana was that kind of person, but this wouldn't be the first time I'd misjudged someone.

I took a deep breath, trying to pull myself together. Then I walked through the doors and headed to Rose's office, greeting my colleagues along the way. During the training period, I was supposed to meet with her every Wednesday to give her an update on my progress.

When I got to the door, though, I heard her talking to someone on the other side. I froze with my hand on the knob. Then, not wanting to interrupt, I took a few steps back and sat on the bench across from her office, swinging my legs while I waited.

At first, I couldn't hear much of what Rose said, and I figured she was on the phone. But at a certain point her voice started rising. There was irritation in her tone, I thought—and suddenly she said her daughter's name.

That was when I heard Diana's voice, loud and clear, and realized Rose wasn't on the phone: She was having a face-to-face argument with her daughter in the room right in front of me.

I didn't catch any full sentences, just bits and pieces.

Not that I was trying to listen in.

I really wasn't.

Their voices got louder and louder, and I shrank into my seat, afraid they would think I was eavesdropping when they opened the door. Especially after last night. I didn't want to see Diana, but somehow I couldn't bring myself to stand up and walk away.

All of a sudden, her voice calmer but still firm and commanding, Rose said something that ended the discussion, period. It was that tone moms use to let you know they're putting their foot down.

"Be at the palace tomorrow at seven. I mean it, Diana."

Palace?!

Their footsteps were coming toward me. I jumped up and sprinted down the hallway, my heart pounding in my ears.

As soon as I rounded the corner, I stopped and took a deep breath. Then I turned around and walked back toward Rose's office as if I'd just arrived.

I took a right and nearly bumped into Diana. When our eyes met, she hesitated, but then her sullen face seemed to relax.

"Hey," she said, seeming genuinely happy to see me.

I was bewildered. She'd given me the cold shoulder just last night, and now she was *smiling* at me? I honestly didn't know what to think. Did the problem have nothing to do with me after all? Was it really about her mom, her escape from the palace, the parts of her life I still knew nothing about?

The only thing I could say for sure was that, after the argument I'd just overheard, there was a huge question mark hovering over her head.

And it was glowing like a neon sign.

What kind of secret is Diana hiding?

"Patrícia, did you know Dayana's in love? She's crazy about—"

I caught up with Emi and clapped a hand over her mouth. Still a little out of breath, she laughed and reached down to pick up the pillow she'd dropped on the floor.

We were at my house, and I'd just threatened to tell her parents that she'd secretly borrowed her mom's real *diamond* jewelry for a date with a girl from one of the fanciest schools in the city. Emi threatened me right back, saying she'd tell my mom that I was in love with Heitor.

Which was a lie. It was just a little crush. A tiny one. About the size of a sinkhole.

When I said, "You would never," she ran into the living room.

"It's not true, Mom!" I insisted, laughing as I pulled Emilly back to my room. "She's just messing with me. You idiot!" I hissed at her when we were back in the hallway.

Later, my mom came to my room and sat on the edge of the bed.

"You know you can tell me if you like someone, right? No matter who it is."

"I know, Mom," I muttered, blushing a little. "It's just a boy from school who I think is cute. It's not a big deal."

"Are you sure?" Her voice was serious.

My heart sped up. What did she mean by that?

"I'm sure, Mom. His name is Heitor."

She hesitated. "Okay, then. That's all I needed."

"What do you mean?"

She stood up and started to sing. "Dayana and Heitor sitting in a tree . . ."

"Mom!"

Chapter 16

When I got off work, my head was spinning. I couldn't stop thinking about Diana and her argument with Rose. It felt like the more pieces I gathered, the less this puzzle made sense.

What did I actually know about Diana?

She was beautiful.

She was a good kisser.

She was sixteen years old and worked at a café in the afternoons and loved watching movies of questionable quality. She was into bands I'd never heard of. She had a Brazilian mom who managed the grocery store where I worked. And she and her mom had been fighting, and for some mysterious reason she'd jumped the fence outside Buckingham Palace one Sunday afternoon.

What if . . . Diana's secret had something to do with the rumors about Prince Arthur?

My eyes widened.

After all, why were they going to the palace the next day?

And why was Rose so set on Diana being there?

Could . . . could *Rose* be the prince's secret lover?

The idea floored me.

Was it really possible? She seemed so down-to-earth, so respectable, that it was hard to believe she'd get involved with a married man in such a public way. And Arthur! I'd always thought he and Tanya were the perfect couple—they were the reason I'd believed in fairy-tale love stories for so long.

But now I knew I couldn't trust men.

My dad was proof of that.

Anyway, it seemed Diana wasn't happy about the whole situation, which must have been why she and Rose were fighting. And based on today's argument, it was clear she was being forced to do something she didn't want to do.

Was Rose the opposite of the model mother I'd imagined?

Was she actually some kind of *con artist*?

Was she trying to use Arthur to steal money from the royal family and give her daughter a better life, but Diana didn't want any part of it?

I shook my head, trying to get a grip on myself. Life in London had obviously filled my head with trash. Of course Rose wasn't a con artist or the prince's secret lover. There had to be a logical explanation I just hadn't thought of yet.

All the same, my mind swirled with questions and theories as I walked toward the Tube station. On an impulse, I pulled out my phone and texted Diana.

Hey, how's it going?

> **You looked a little down earlier**

Would she figure out I'd been eavesdropping? I chewed distractedly on one of my nails while I waited for her response. She started typing, then stopped. I watched *Typing* appear and disappear multiple times before the phone finally vibrated.

> **It's no big deal, just something with my mom**

> **We're not in a great place right now**

> **I thought you made up?**

> **We did, but we fought again today**

I stared at my phone, wondering how to respond.

> **Ugh, that sucks**

> **If you ever want to talk about it**

> **I'm here for you**

> **Thank you ☺**

The online status below her name vanished. I jiggled my leg nervously.

I was beyond curious, but I also had no way of making her tell the truth. What could I do? Ask her directly and admit that I'd listened in on her conversation?

I was so tired, both mentally and physically, that when I got home all I wanted to do was turn off my brain and fall into bed. But when I opened my bedroom door, I found Georgia lying there, flipping through *Everything Leads to You*, which she'd taken from my nightstand. I hadn't gotten around to reading it back in Brazil, but when I was packing, I decided to pull it off the shelf and bring it with me for English practice.

"Ugh, I'm starting to rethink this whole getting-along-with-you thing," I moaned, dropping my bag and collapsing on the floor.

"Bad day?" she asked, leaning over the edge of the bed to examine me.

"No, everything's fine," I said, a tinge of annoyance in my voice.

"How's Diana?"

I hesitated.

I hadn't planned on telling Georgia anything, but ... maybe she could help me figure out what to do. Or at least bring me back down to Earth.

So I told her everything.

When I repeated what Rose had said to Diana, Georgia sprang up on the bed and landed on all fours, her mouth hanging open.

"Bloody hell, Dayana!"

"Shhh!" I hissed, gesturing at her to keep it down. Telling Georgia was one thing, but I didn't want Lauren breathing down my neck. I got the sense that she was the neighborhood loudmouth. "Stop yelling!"

"Bloody hell," she repeated, this time in a whisper. "Dayana, you're dating the daughter of Prince Arthur's lover! This is the juiciest gossip ever!"

I rolled my eyes, but I couldn't help laughing. When Georgia said it out loud like that, it sounded completely absurd.

"I don't know if it's true, though. Like, can we actually trust the tabloids? Their story doesn't even make sense. Why would Arthur bring his lover to Buckingham Palace? Maybe Rose is just doing some kind of work for the royal family. Like catering an event or something? And Diana doesn't want to help her, and that's why they're fighting."

With every word, I felt more and more convinced. Yes, this was the most logical explanation. Definitely. So maybe the truth was nothing at all like what I'd imagined earlier.

"But why would she keep that a secret?"

I thought for a minute. "Confidentiality clause? An NDA?"

Georgia pursed her lips. "I don't know . . . it's all pretty strange."

She lay back down and we both fell silent, mulling over the possibilities.

After a while, my stomach rumbled and I stood up.

"Well, there's nothing I can do now except wait—and eat. I'm starving."

We followed a delicious aroma into the kitchen. I glanced at the various pots and pans, expecting to find our usual dinner: rice, canned beans, vegetables, and meat. Instead, I was surprised to see a pressure cooker on the counter, giving off the unmistakable scent of corn. On the stove, a glass bowl wrapped in a dish towel rested above a pot of boiling water.

"Is that couscous?" I asked in amazement. I tried to peek under the dish towel, but Lauren gently slapped my hand away.

"Get out of there, you'll throw off the process!" There was laughter in her voice, so I didn't take it too seriously. I was already inspecting a third pot, which was full of boiled plantains. All my favorite afternoon snacks. "Stop poking around, amor. Go sit down."

"What *is* all this?"

"I went to the Brazilian market today. I thought it would be nice to make some classic treats from back home, the ones you like best, so you don't get too homesick."

I was touched. "How did you know I liked all these things?"

"I talked to your grandparents." Lauren shrugged, as if it wasn't a big deal.

But it was huge.

Before I knew it, I was hugging her. "You're the best, Lauren."

She patted my arm, slightly disconcerted. "It's nothing, querida. Go wash your hands and sit down."

I turned around to find Georgia watching us, an odd look on her face. The hug had been a surprise to all of us, me included, but what could I do? Lauren was winning me over with food. She was kind to me.

I shrugged, a little embarrassed, and took a seat next to Georgia.

We sat in silence for a while—I mean, Georgia and I did, because Lauren was chattering away about everything she'd bought at the market. And then Georgia leaned toward me.

I jumped at her sudden movement.

"I have an idea," she whispered. "About how we can find out what's up with your girl."

If her sly smile was any indication, I wasn't sure I was going to like this idea.

"Don't you think it's kind of weird that he doesn't want any-one to know you're hooking up?" Emi and I were sitting together in a corner during our free period.

The previous weekend, she, Lara, and I had gone to a classmate's house for a party. During a game of truth or dare, I'd had my first kiss with Heitor, the guy I'd liked since the start of the school year. Yes, it sucked that we'd first hooked up on a dare. But that was how I got him to notice me.

At school the next day, he pulled me into a corner and kissed me again.

I felt like I'd died and gone to heaven. Only Emi and Lara knew this, but that night at the party was the first time I'd ever kissed anyone. It had been incredible, but it was even better to find out that he'd liked it, too—so much that he wanted more.

When I tried to talk to him in the classroom on Tuesday, though, Heitor ignored me. Later, during free period, he brought me to an empty hallway and started making out with me again.

It didn't make any sense.

"It's just that if the other guys start talking, it'll ruin this great thing we have," he explained when I asked why he'd been so rude to me.

Emi and Lara were not amused.

"I don't know, Day, something seems off." Lara thought

for a moment. "People only keep secrets like that when they have something to be ashamed of. And if he's ashamed of you, he'd better watch out, because I will personally kick him in the balls."

"Innocent until proven guilty, right?" I laughed, trying to dismiss the idea, even though it had occurred to me, too. "Give him a break."

Because why would he hook up with me if he was ashamed of me? And what was so wrong with keeping it on the DL? Everyone had secrets. It didn't mean anything.

Chapter 17

Rose didn't show up at Sugar's Grocery the next day.

My mind wandered all through my shift, and my eyes flicked constantly from the wall clock to my wristwatch to the little numbers on the inventory computer screen. When I sat down, I jiggled my leg subconsciously, and my stomach felt like the Bermuda Triangle: Everything I ate seemed to mysteriously disappear because I'd scarfed it all down so quickly.

When the clock struck six, I threw on my street clothes and ran out the door without even saying goodbye to my colleagues. At the Tube station, I found the line I needed and hopped on the first train to Green Park, the stop closest to the palace.

My phone pinged with a message from Georgia.

Are you on your way?

Yep

More soon

She'd wanted to come with me, obviously—we were both dying to know what Diana was up to. But in the end, because of her health issues, she thought she might just get in the way, so she decided to stay home and cover for me. I'd told Lauren and Roberto I was filling in for a colleague who worked the late shift, but then, out of nowhere, my dad had offered to pick me up afterward. Of all the times to act like a father, he had to choose *this* one?

So, the plan was: Scope out the palace and see if I could spot Rose or Diana arriving. Stick around until the end of my supposed shift. Then head back to the grocery store in time for Roberto to pick me up.

When I heard "Green Park" over the speaker, I got up and pushed through the packed car to the doors. It was rush hour, and I got swept up in the crowd. With all its zigzagging staircases, the station was a little overwhelming, but luckily I was able to follow the signs.

When the claustrophobic tunnels finally spat me out aboveground, the London wind hit me full in the face.

I headed to the front of the palace to stake out the entrance. I looked at my watch; it was almost seven. The Royal Standard was flying high, which meant the Queen was at home. Could Rose have already arrived? After all, the English were known for their punctuality. Would she have come by car or on foot? Would she have used a back door?

I pulled out my phone and texted Georgia.

I'm here

Waiting

All good there?

She was supposed to keep an eye on Roberto and let me know if he decided to leave early.

I leaned against the foot of the Victoria Memorial, waiting.

Even after seven, no one showed up.

A strange feeling took hold of me.

What was I hoping to achieve here?

If I found out that Rose really was the prince's secret lover, what would it change? What would I do with that knowledge?

Suddenly, I felt ridiculous.

Was I here because I couldn't help sticking my nose in other people's business? Or because . . .

No.

I deserved the truth.

Diana couldn't keep toying with me like this, dangling hints in front of me only to yank them away. If she wouldn't tell me, I would figure it out on my own.

To distract myself from the questions multiplying in my

head, I set out to trace the palace perimeter and look for gaps in the fence. I wasn't trying to *break in* or anything. I just wanted to observe, to see if I could learn anything new. A glimpse of a window, maybe? A conversation between palace staff?

I followed the wrought iron fence, scanning Buckingham's timeworn walls. How old was the palace? Centuries, probably. Even so, the building looked solid, its paint job flawless. I was always surprised by how well London was maintained. The streets were super clean, and all the old buildings were carefully preserved. I wished I could say the same about the historic center of Rio.

Which reminded me how much I missed my city. The beaches, the view of Christ the Redeemer when I took Rebouças Tunnel toward the South Zone. I even missed complaining about the heat and the earthy taste of geosmin in the water. (To be honest, London water didn't taste all that great, either, though apparently it was highly treated.) I missed my cozy bedroom, the room that actually felt like *mine*, and the warm scent of my grandparents when I hugged them every morning.

I found myself on a dimly lit stretch of sidewalk where the fence gave way to reinforced walls. It was the exact spot where I'd first met Diana. I stopped and peered over my shoulder. I'd been so absorbed in my thoughts, I hadn't been paying attention to my surroundings.

But before I could start moving again, I heard quick foot-steps coming toward me. I looked at the fence. The museum banner blocked my view of the other side, but I glimpsed a pair of feet. Then the person started climbing.

Oh no, not again.

It all happened so fast.

I tried to step back in time, but yet again, the escapee landed right on top of me, knocking me to the ground in a knot of arms and legs. When I opened my eyes, my heart pounding like crazy, a lock of silky red hair was tickling my nose. Then a white, freckled face came into focus, and there they were—four little dots shaped like the Southern Cross.

Diana stared at me in astonishment. "Dayana?!"

Un-effing-believable. Talk about déjà vu.

I opened my mouth, then shut it again when I realized nothing was going to come out. Because how could I possibly explain what I was doing there? The gravity of what I'd done hit me like a ton of bricks. I'd overheard her talking with her mom and decided to spy on her. *What a shitty thing to do, Dayana.*

Before she could ask what the hell I was doing there, we heard hurried footsteps in the distance. Startled, Diana peered through the fence and then jumped to her feet. For a second, I thought she was going to take off running, leaving me sprawled out on the sidewalk—which I definitely would have deserved.

Instead, she reached out a hand and helped me up.

"Come on. We have to get out of here" was all she said. Then she started sprinting, my hand still in hers.

We ran along the palace wall as quietly as we could, crossing at the same intersection and turning down the same side street as last time.

I watched her from the corner of my eye. She was dressed in simple business casual, not her style at all. Black jeans. A white, tucked-in button-down shirt that was stained in a few places. Hair in a bun.

Her black combat boots were the only thing that felt like *her*, though they clashed with the rest of her outfit.

She looked up at me, and our eyes met. She was probably confused about my being there, and maybe annoyed by the intrusion. But nothing in her face gave any indication of what was going through her head.

Before I could say anything, I ran into someone and almost fell. Diana slowed down so I could regain my balance. As I sidestepped the tall, pale man I'd bumped into, I noticed his cheeks flushing an angry red.

"Sorry!" I yelled over my shoulder, trying to make an apologetic face while also running at a reasonable speed.

I looked forward again, and Diana picked up the pace.

The farther we got from the palace, and the deeper we went into the maze of alleyways, the more the city came to life. Businessmen in starched suits chatted cheerfully as they left their offices, probably heading to a nearby pub to unwind. Two girls a little older than Diana and me, both dressed for a night out, laughed loudly as they passed; one had an orangey fake tan, while the other wore impossibly high heels. We slowed down to dodge big groups on the sidewalk, sometimes jumping off the curb and into the street.

I was almost out of breath when I spotted the Palace of Westminster and, soon after, the River Thames, as long and shiny as it had been on that Sunday with Roberto. My legs ached, and I was panting—I'd barely done any exercise since the beginning of the year. I was very out of shape.

When we reached Westminster Bridge, Diana slowed us down to a calm walking pace. We were far enough away now. She let go of my hand, and my heart clenched into a little ball. But since we hadn't come to a full stop yet, I kept my mouth shut.

I glanced at Diana. She was frowning at me, her eyes narrowed. A few strands of hair had escaped her perfect bun and now stuck to her sweaty temples, framing her face.

She was breathing hard, her chest rising and falling quickly.

I felt exposed under her gaze and looked away. Was she mad at me?

We passed the crowded London Eye, the line stretching so far I couldn't see where it ended. Ahead of us was Hungerford Bridge, with those unmistakable white pyramids jutting up along the sides. A train rattled by above our heads when we crossed it.

By the time we stopped, the sky had paled. Diana leaned over the Thames, her elbows on the wall dividing the sidewalk from the murky water below. There were a few people around, some strolling or exercising in the breeze off the river, others lying on benches and soaking up the last rays of sun. It was much quieter here than in the touristy parts of the city we'd left behind.

No one paid us any attention.

I looked at her.

"I'm sorry," I said, before she could get a word in.

She stared at me. "What the hell were you doing there?"

I shrank from the indignation in her voice.

"It can't just be a coincidence. Not again."

"I heard you talking with your mom," I admitted, also in English, as a sign of respect. Or maybe because it was easier to tell the truth in another language. "About going to . . ." I looked around and lowered my voice. "The palace." I straightened up and cleared my throat. "I know I shouldn't have come. It was really invasive. But . . . after what I heard, you can't blame me for being curious. Remember how we met? What else could I have done?"

"You could have trusted me! You could have *talked* to me, told me you were worried I was a criminal or whatever."

"And would you have told me the truth?"

"Maybe. But I doubt it." She nodded for emphasis. "So that's it, huh? Since I wasn't going to tell you, you went and spied on me? You're always telling me how hard it is to live with your dad's family because they don't respect your privacy. But here you are doing the exact same thing!" She let out a humorless laugh, her words dripping with scorn.

When she turned her back on me, I started panicking.

Diana was right. Of course she was. The moment she'd looked at me with those frightened green eyes, there on the sidewalk outside the palace, I'd realized how wrong I was. And it had dawned on me exactly what was going on here: I was sabotaging myself. Everything was going so well that I'd had to make a mess of it somehow.

I grabbed her arm desperately, trying to keep her from walking away.

"I'm sorry." I let her go and pressed my palms together as if in prayer, but without breaking eye contact. "I'm so sorry. I'm so, so sorry. I know I messed up. I got scared because you were acting so distant and I knew something was going on in your life and . . . I don't know, I just freaked out."

My eyes welled up with tears.

Diana ran her fingers through her auburn hair, seemingly unsure what to do, before taking my hand and pulling me to an empty bench by the water. But she didn't sit down. She paced back and forth, combing a hand through her hair, a troubled look on her face. My heart sank. The next time she passed me, I reached for her hand.

"I'm sorry," I said again. "I'm really sorry. I don't need to know. I trust you." And I meant it. "All I want is for you to trust me back. You don't have to tell me your secret. Just don't ghost me when things get hard. If you pull away whenever something bad happens, there's a good chance I'll get all worked up again."

Diana studied me, tears glistening in her eyes. Then she sighed and sat down beside me, still holding my hand. Looking down at our interlaced fingers, she smiled sadly. She was silent for so long I didn't think she would say anything.

Then, in English, she began, "You told me your dad left when you were six years old. I could relate, because I never even met my dad." She squeezed my hand, as if gathering her courage. "My mom said he'd died in a car accident, but as I got older, her story seemed more and more suspicious. She didn't have any photos of him, or any of his things." Frustration crept into her voice. "I tried to look for him a few times—news articles, an obituary, that kind of thing—but I never found anything."

The breeze from the river picked up, blowing my hair into my face. I had to drop Diana's hand to slip an elastic off my wrist and put it up in a ponytail. When the wind tossed a lock of hair into her eyes, she tucked it behind her ear. The strands around her forehead were still sweaty from our run. I took her hand again, wishing I'd never have to let it go.

She didn't pull away.

"We were living in Brighton, and my mom almost never took me to London. Sometimes I felt like we were running away . . ." She trailed off, her voice thick with emotion.

"But you came here in the end," I added encouragingly.

Diana nodded. "Yeah, we moved here two years ago. My mom was the assistant manager of the Sugar's Grocery back in Brighton. When a job opened up at the London branch, she applied, even though there was a lot of competition. I don't know why she decided it was the right time, but she got the job and we moved. Maybe because enough time had passed—"

"Enough time for what?" I interrupted.

And what does this have to do with the royal family? I didn't say it out loud, obviously—I would respect whatever Diana wanted to tell me. I didn't exactly have the moral high ground here.

Diana looked at me.

"For people to have forgotten." She hesitated for a while, clearly torn about whether to go on. Then she said, "The day we met, I was running because I'd just found out my dad was not only alive, but also . . ."

I held my breath.

"An actual prince."

Chapter 18

"No way. You're messing with me, right?"

I smiled uncertainly, my head cocked. This had to be a joke. There couldn't be any truth in my desperate, half-baked theories. But Diana gave me a sympathetic half smile. I wasn't sure if she'd understood my Portuguese slang, but she couldn't have missed the disbelief in my voice.

She just kept looking at me until I realized she was one hundred percent serious.

"But . . . but . . . how?!"

She held up her hands, palms facing the sky.

"I'm still trying to figure that out." She ran a hand through her hair, freeing more strands from her already disheveled bun. "All I know is that my mom met the prince in college and . . . well, I was born. I'm not really sure what happened after that. She says she didn't want to get involved in all the royal drama, but I think there's something she's not telling me. Why did she drop out and run away without telling him she was pregnant? And if she wanted nothing to do with the royals, why did she change her mind a few weeks ago? Why did she tell them everything and ask for a DNA test? None of it makes sense, but honestly, the main thing I'm trying to process is that my dad is alive and my mom lied to me my whole life." Her voice edged toward hysteria, and almost without realizing it, I squeezed her hand tighter. "She didn't have any right to keep this from me!"

I could see the anguish in her eyes. When the tears broke free and ran down her cheeks, she hid her face from me and rubbed her eyes fiercely. But the tears kept falling.

I felt a deep connection between us, a shared pain. We'd both lost our fathers and then had to deal with their sudden return. I was grieving my mom's death; she was grieving the story she'd believed all her life. It wasn't the same thing, but something had broken in both of us. Being with Diana didn't exactly make me feel whole—I'd never say something that cliché. But we helped put each other back together and feel like ourselves again, despite the scars.

In fact, we'd met at the exact moment we needed each other most.

I squeezed her hand, and she looked up at me. Our eyes met. *Don't worry, it's okay. I'm right here.*

Her shoulders relaxed, and she gazed out over the Thames again.

"What about today? What happened?" I ventured. I didn't want to seem *too* interested, but after a story like that, I couldn't help myself.

"Today we got the results. Of the paternity test."

"And was it . . ." I paused. "Positive?"

She forced her lips into another pained smile. "Of course."

"*Damn.* So . . . what now?" I asked quietly.

She shrugged. "I don't know, I didn't stick around to hear the details. But I don't want any of it. That life isn't for me, you know? I don't want anyone to find out, and I don't even want his money, even though it's his legal obligation and my mom deserves it after raising me alone for all this time. It's her fault he wasn't involved in my life, but it's partly his fault I was born in the first place. So . . . I don't know." Diana sighed. "All I wanted was a dad. I just wish I hadn't spent my whole life thinking he was dead, only to discover sixteen years later that he's very much alive and living in a palace. I don't know how to handle it."

"I understand a lot better than I'd like to," I said, trying to comfort her. "I mean, the part about suddenly having a dad again. Not the part about being the daughter of . . . Prince Arthur." I smiled sheepishly, and she laughed a little. "It won't be easy, but at least he's open to it. Who knows, maybe he actually *wants* to take on the responsibility. You can't make up for lost time, but you can have a future together. Though in my case, that's where things get a bit more complicated . . ."

Diana raised her eyebrows. She always said I was too stubborn when it came to my dad. But this was about her, not me, so I ignored the implication.

"And I get how mad you are at your mom," I continued, "but I also get why she wouldn't want to be mixed up with the royal family. King Oliver was always super traditional and conservative. Maybe she was scared something would happen?" I added, lowering my voice.

Diana nodded. "Yeah, maybe." She paused and looked at me. "I know this goes without saying, but for god's sake, Day, this *needs* to stay between us. You have to *promise* you won't tell anyone. It's a state secret. Literally!" The joke made me fall even more in love with her. As if I wasn't already head over heels. "I shouldn't have even told you."

"Don't worry, my lips are sealed." I mimed zipping my mouth shut. "But why did you tell me? I think we both agree I don't deserve it."

"What you said before, about trusting you back . . . you were right. And I do trust you. Even after what happened today, I feel like I can confide in you. It sounds stupid, but you know when you get along so well with someone it's like you've known each other forever?"

I did know, because it was exactly how I felt.

"We have an expression for that in Portuguese, but I don't know if it translates."

Diana tilted her head. "What is it?"

"Nosso santo bateu. It's like . . . our saints match." I grinned. "I feel the same way about you. When I got to London, I was feeling so hopeless . . . it was amazing to meet someone I could talk to and laugh with and be myself with, you know? I didn't think I would ever feel that good again after my mom died."

"I totally get it. I was feeling so . . . so lost, that day we met. When I found out the truth. It felt like my whole life was a lie and I didn't know who I was anymore. And then you appeared."

My heart sped up. The loneliness of the last two months felt like a distant memory. Maybe Diana was an angel sent by my mom.

She took a lock of hair that had slipped from my ponytail and tucked it behind my ear, her eyes fixed on mine. From that close, I could tell her green irises were a shade darker around the rim. Her bun had come loose, the orangey strands tousled by the wind, and I felt an urge to smooth them back into place.

Diana studied my face, as if she wanted to memorize my brown skin, my full cheeks, my dark eyes. I bit my lip nervously. Her gaze darted to my mouth, and suddenly it was like all the blood in my veins evaporated.

Diana smiled and leaned in for a kiss.

That was when it hit me.

I was in love with Prince Arthur's long-lost daughter.

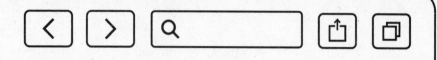

Palace Intrigue: Another Meeting Behind Closed Doors

by Chloe Ward

The royals aren't exactly discreet when it comes to family gatherings and political meetings. Quite the opposite: As a rule, palace events are showy and extravagant. But recently the comings and goings at Buckingham have been kept under wraps—and no one knows why.

Rumor has it that Prince Arthur and Tanya Parekh's relationship is increasingly strained, perhaps because the mysterious woman who's been meeting with the Duke of York returned to the palace on Thursday.

Until the palace makes an official announcement, all we can do is speculate: Are we headed toward another royal divorce?

Chapter 19

"Do you have any idea how irresponsible that was, Dayana?" Roberto's voice thundered through the house. His face was red, and the veins pulsed in his neck. He paced from one side of the living room to the other, truly angry for the first time since I'd arrived.

I was sitting on the couch, listening to his lecture with my head held high. Yes, I'd made a mistake. I hadn't noticed how late it was until the London Eye and the buildings along the Thames lit up. The effect was magical: Under the violet sky, the lights reflected yellow, orange, blue, and red on the dark river, like in a watercolor painting. It reminded me of the nighttime view of Rodrigo de Freitas Lagoon at Christmastime, the huge tree in the middle of the lake glowing with joyful multicolored lights. But I was too startled to enjoy the view.

I pulled out my phone, my heart racing, and found a ton of missed calls and unread messages. It was past nine, which was when Roberto was supposed to pick me up at the grocery store.

As Diana and I ran to the Tube, I scrolled through Georgia's messages.

All good?

Hello?

Hey, our dad's getting ready

Where are you????

Dayana HE'S COMING

YOU BETTER BE ON THE WAY

Oh shit

Your coworkers snitched on you

He's running around looking for you

My mom was bugging me so I said you were with a boy

SORRY

> Oh god, I hope you're ok

> I hope you didn't do anything stupid

> Please just say something, I'm worried about you

When I finally got home, Lauren and Roberto were pacing back and forth in front of Georgia, who was huddled on the couch.

Okay, I got the point. I knew everyone was worried about me. I knew I'd been careless. But I refused to hang my head in front of the man who'd given up being my dad.

Beside me, though, Georgia stared at her feet.

"Do you think just because you're not in Brazil anymore, you can do whatever you want? That London is some kind of fairy-tale world? Because it isn't!" His voice rose. "Something could have happened! And you, Georgia, covering for her? I'm so disappointed."

Georgia shrank into the couch cushions.

"Do you know how I felt when I got there and found out you'd been gone for hours?" he went on. "That you'd *lied* to me?"

Anger bubbled up in me like boiling water. The same anger that had been simmering for the past few days, while I started to get used to this new life, this new family.

"Give me a break! What about *you*?" I roared back,

quivering with rage. "You think just because I'm here now, under your roof, that you're my dad again? Where were *you* when I was sick and my mom had to stay up all night taking care of me? Where were you when she pulled all-nighters to support us on her own? WHERE WERE YOU WHEN SHE DIED?"

I thought that would stop him in his tracks like it had the first time. I thought he'd tense up and start spluttering. But apparently I'd underestimated his fury, because the vein in his neck only pulsed harder and he puffed out his chest aggressively.

"It doesn't matter what happened in the past. You're my responsibility *now*, and you have to follow my rules!"

Lauren took a step toward him and put a hand on his shoulder. Even she seemed a little scared. At our feet, Ruffles started barking nervously.

"Take it easy, amor," Lauren said. It was like I'd fallen into Alice's rabbit hole and now everything was upside down. Roberto in a rage, Lauren trying to smooth things over. "The girls made a mistake, but what matters is that Dayana's okay."

"But what if she wasn't?!"

"It doesn't matter what happened in the past?" I broke in, ignoring Lauren's attempt at peacemaking. "Maybe you've been fine without us for all this time, but you have no idea how many times I needed you! Where was your *concern*"—I made air quotes just to piss him off—"these past ten years?"

192

The more grievances I threw at him, the angrier he got. And the more he vented his rage, the more irrational I became.

"You have no idea what I've been through!" he countered.

"If you hadn't left us, maybe I would!"

He took a deep breath.

"End of discussion. You're grounded. And you too!" he said to Georgia. "And would you shut up?!" he yelled at the dog, who drew back with a whimper.

"What?" Georgia asked, horrified.

"Oh, for god's sake . . ." I said at the same time.

"If you complain, I'll confiscate your phones, too," he interrupted. "To your rooms! No dillydallying."

"Don't worry, I'm going!" I yelled. "I can't stand to look at you for another second."

I stomped to my room and slammed the door, but the anger didn't go away. I wanted to smash everything I could get my hands on, but a little voice in my head—which sounded a lot like my mom—told me it wouldn't do any good; it would only make things worse for me.

I flopped onto my bed, wrapping my arms around the pillow. The tears started flowing. I couldn't believe that when I'd finally managed to say all the things that had been stuck in my throat for so long, Roberto had had the nerve to get mad at me. I'd pictured this scene so many times, but in my imagination, he almost always broke down crying and apologized to me. Sometimes I forgave him, other times I didn't. When I felt especially depressed, I imagined him saying coldly that he didn't regret anything and that he'd only taken me back because he'd had no other choice.

But I'd never, *ever* imagined he would get angry.

Who did he think he was to tell *me* I had no idea what he'd been through?

I had a pretty good idea, actually: He'd met someone else and started a new, less complicated family to replace the old one, which had stayed behind. And he'd had a high standard of living.

He was crazy if he thought I was going to sympathize with his supposedly hard life.

A gentle knock interrupted my negative spiral.

"Don't worry, Day, I'll talk to him." Lauren's muffled voice came through the closed door. "He was just worried, but he'll calm down, I promise."

I didn't answer. Her footsteps faded away, leaving the house in silence. My fierce sobs—a mix of anger, sadness, and grief—were the only sound. I cried until I didn't have any tears left.

I felt so adrift. So lost. How could I live in that house for two more years? How could I look Roberto in the eye every day after the fight we'd just had? It wasn't our first, and it definitely wouldn't be our last.

I eventually dozed off and was woken a while later by another knock at the door.

"Day?" It was Georgia. She opened the door a crack. "Can I come in?"

I sat up in bed and rubbed my eyes, which were swollen from so much crying.

"Yeah."

She tiptoed in and sat on the edge of my bed. I looked at my phone and saw that it was almost two in the morning. She must have waited for Lauren and Roberto to fall asleep before sneaking down to my room.

"Are you in pain again?" I asked, seeing the face she made when she shifted her weight.

"A little. I've been good the last few days, but it started again tonight."

"Really?" I frowned. "Do you think it's, like, a psychological thing?"

She rolled her eyes. "It's not psychological if I actually *feel* pain."

"Sorry," I said, holding my hands up. "I meant psychosomatic. You know, when an emotional issue takes a toll on your body. Take my grandma. She was really sick after . . . you know."

She grimaced. "I don't know, I hadn't thought of that. I've done some research online, but it could be a million different things."

"Maybe you should go to a psychiatrist? A pain specialist or a rheumatologist or a chiropractor. My grandparents are really into all that stuff."

She cocked her head. "Are you calling me old?"

I giggled, and the tension between us dissolved.

"Are *you* okay?" Georgia asked after a while.

I just shrugged, and we sat there in silence for a few minutes while I woke up from my not-so-restorative sleep. The fight with Roberto was still fresh in my mind.

"You could have pretended you didn't know anything," I said at last. "You didn't have to go down with me."

She laughed, but in a slightly unsettling way. "I didn't think it was fair for you to get all the blame when it was my idea."

I looked at her, grateful for the support.

"And I wanted to say sorry," she went on glumly. "It was actually a terrible idea. I've been having a hard time lately because it feels like this pain won't go away, it just keeps getting worse. Maybe I was trying to live through you . . ." She attempted a smile, her eyes downcast. "But what happened in the end? Did you find anything out?"

I wrinkled my brow. The argument with Roberto had swept everything else from my mind. But as I went over the day's events, from the palace stakeout to my second escape with Diana, the prince's daughter—*the prince's daughter!*—the adrenaline came back at full blast.

I hesitated. Diana had asked me to keep my mouth shut, and

I understood why. This wasn't a joke. For the first time, I saw how serious it was: Queen Diana's son, the freaking *prince*, had an illegitimate daughter, and based on what I'd read in the tabloids, this fact was putting a real strain on Arthur's marriage. If the news got out, it would be a *massive* scandal. And Diana would be caught in the eye of the storm.

"I promised I wouldn't tell anyone," I said uncertainly.

I should have lied and told her no, I hadn't found anything out. But I wasn't thinking straight.

Georgia grabbed my hands and stared at me with giant puppy-dog eyes.

"I'm not just anyone, I'm your *sister*. It won't leave this room."

Hearing Georgia call herself my sister gave me a strange satisfaction. I almost grinned. She'd had my back through all this craziness, and without her, I wouldn't have learned anything. When the plan fell apart, she'd stood by me and taken her share of the blame. Didn't she deserve the truth? And hadn't Diana agreed that we needed to trust each other?

I squeezed Georgia's hands, returning her enthusiasm as if I hadn't just had a huge fight with my dad.

"Listen, Georgia," I whispered. "You can't tell *anyone*, okay? I mean it. You can't tell your mom, or Roberto, or your best friend."

Her eyes widened. "It's that serious?"

I nodded.

Then I told her everything.

Chapter 20

"How long have you been glued to that phone, querida?" Lauren poked her head out the kitchen door with a friendly smile.

I was curled up on the love seat on the back porch, my arms around my knees. The sun had been shining all morning, but there in the shade, the wind made the hair on my arms stand up. Ruffles ran through the grass, chasing every bird that dared to invade his territory. I'd managed to avoid Roberto at breakfast, but the bare walls of my room had started to get on my nerves, and I was too scared of running into him to stay in the living room. So I'd ended up taking refuge in the yard for the first time since moving to London.

I'd never lived in a *house* house, so I wasn't used to having a porch or such a big, open outdoor space to relax in. It felt good to escape my claustrophobic room and listen to the birds chirping in the trees. The house was in a quiet residential neighborhood, and there was barely any noise from the street. Back in Brazil, cars and buses rattled by my window all day, every day.

I put the phone to sleep and looked up at Lauren.

"I'm not glued to my phone," I said, less convincingly than I would have liked.

I still hadn't heard anything from Diana, and I wondered if she'd been grounded, too. It was the second time she'd run away from the palace, and Rose hadn't seemed very understanding in the conversation I'd overheard. Which was ridiculous: After all, she was the one who'd lied in the first place.

I texted her a *Hey, what's up?*, partly because I was worried but also because I felt a little guilty about sharing her secret, even if it was only with Georgia. It felt like any minute now a giant red sign with the words PROMISE BREAKER scrawled on it would pop up over my head.

To ease my conscience, I checked a few different gossip sites. I couldn't find anything about Prince Arthur having an illegitimate daughter, or even any updates about his supposed infidelity. It was crazy how shameless the tabloids were. The slightest suspicion ended up on the front page.

No messages, no leaked secrets. I just sat there, waiting. And staring at my phone.

"Is it the boy from yesterday?" Lauren asked, sitting down beside me on the love seat.

I still wasn't sure if I could trust Lauren with something like this. True, she'd tried to calm Roberto down the day before, but was it just because she'd been startled by his overreaction? Or did she honestly not think it was that big a deal?

"It's nothing. I'm just enjoying the morning breeze." The excuse sounded fake even to me.

She looked at me skeptically.

"You can trust me, amor." She put her hand on mine in a motherly way. "I won't tell your dad, I promise. I know he got carried away yesterday. You didn't have to lie, claro, and he was right that something could have happened, but I understand why you didn't tell us. And I trust you to make good decisions."

I looked at her. Lauren was smiling at me expectantly. My thoughts turned to my mom. We hadn't had many talks like this, and I'd never had a chance to tell her I was bi. I was with Heitor before she died, and I used that to hide the truth.

There were so many things I wished I'd told her.

I took a deep breath.

"It's . . . actually a girl," I said timidly.

"Oh." Lauren didn't try to conceal her surprise. She blinked, absorbing the information. "Okay, não tem problema. We don't discriminate in this house. You love who you love."

She squeezed my hand, and I felt strangely grateful. I could tell she wasn't one hundred percent comfortable with this conversation, but her reaction was a lot better than I'd expected.

"Is she the one you were with yesterday?"

I nodded.

"Okay," she said slowly. "And you're . . . you're . . . you know . . ." She gestured vaguely with her hands. "Using protection?"

My jaw dropped.

"Lauren!" I exclaimed, the color rising to my cheeks.

"What?" She held up her hands. "Pregnancy isn't the only unwanted consequence of unprotected sex—"

"Oh my god."

"There are forms of protection for women who have sex with women, too, and it's important that you know—"

"Lauren!" I said more loudly, my face burning with embarrassment. "Don't worry, I'm a virgin!"

"But sometimes these things happen spontaneously," she went on, and I wanted to dig a hole in the ground and bury myself in it. "You should make sure you're educated. If you want me to—"

"No thanks! I can do my own research. Just leave it to me," I cut in before she could say more.

She hesitated. "So why have you been looking at your phone?"

Since I couldn't be totally honest, I opted for part of the truth. "I just want to know if she's okay. I'm worried her mom might have grounded her, too."

Lauren clicked her tongue reprovingly. "You kids need to learn to trust people. Adults don't bite, you know."

I couldn't help laughing, and she joined in, making me feel unexpectedly close to her. Who would have thought that one day I'd be opening up to *Lauren* of all people?

Times change, I guess.

"Mom?" Georgia called tentatively from inside the house.

"I'm out here!"

Georgia appeared in the doorway.

She looked from her mom to me and back again, a strange expression flashing across her face. Could she be . . . jealous? Of me? For having a friendly one-on-one conversation with her mom? It wasn't the first time I'd seen that look in her eyes.

But this was normal, wasn't it? I'd seen a bunch of Emi's and Lara's fights with their sisters, and the worst ones were always about jealousy.

But as an only child, I'd never had to deal with any of that.

"I'm ready," Georgia said in English, and I noticed she'd changed out of her pajamas into jeans and a T-shirt.

Lauren patted my leg.

"Great chat, sweetie," she said in English, then stood up, satisfied with our talk.

They went on their way, and I heard the front door close behind them.

I was surprised to feel slightly left out. I mean, I knew they were only going to the store, but it hadn't even occurred to them to invite me?

The thought made my eyes bug out. Was *I* jealous of Georgia? Oh my god. What was London doing to me?

Suddenly, Ruffles's leaps through the grass didn't seem so charming anymore. I decided to go sulk in my room.

That was when I ran into Roberto.

He was blocking my way, so I took a step back. For the first time, he didn't try to smooth things over by pretending nothing had happened.

"Good morning," he said quietly. He didn't meet my eyes.

"Good morning," I responded, a hint of annoyance in my voice.

I tried to slip past him, but he took a step in the same direction, so I couldn't get by. He seemed uncomfortable. I crossed my arms and waited. For him to apologize? Restart the fight? At least say *something*?

Or maybe I was gathering my courage. I'd thrown a lot of blame at him the night before, but we hadn't exactly had the conversation I'd always imagined. And I hadn't asked any of the questions that had been on my mind.

Was he happy? Did he ever miss us? His ex-wife, his ex-family, his ex-life? Did he ever regret leaving and not looking back?

He stepped to the side, clearing my path.

Neither of us said a thing.

My heart was pounding as I held the phone to my ear. So many years had passed, but I still felt like that same seven-year-old calling her father, full of excitement, only to find another girl calling him Dad on the other end.

Someone picked up, and I held my breath. Ever since that first time, calling Roberto made me break out in a cold sweat. I was always afraid I'd have to deal with Lauren or Georgia.

"Hello?" a velvety voice said in English.

It was Georgia.

I squeezed the phone tighter.

"Hi, can I talk to Roberto?" I asked in English.

"Who is this?" Her voice was haughty.

"His daughter."

She went to find him, and I sighed with relief.

A minute or so later, Roberto picked up.

"Hey, Dayana! How are you doing, baby girl?" The same cheerful voice as always. As if he didn't have a care in the world.

"I'm good, how are you?"

"Better now that I'm talking to you!" I could tell he was smiling on the other end. "What's up?"

"I, uh . . ."

"Is that Dayana?" someone asked in the background.

"It is!"

"Hi, querida!" Lauren said in that singsongy voice of hers. "We haven't heard from you in a while! When are

204

you going to come visit? We'd love to have you here."

I looked at my mom, who was standing in the hallway. She raised her eyebrows. Lauriane? *she mouthed. I rolled my eyes and nodded.*

"Oh, I'm not sure, Lauren. Money is kind of tight right now. You know how it is." I couldn't resist a little jab.

If it was up to me, I'd never visit them. Or at least never go to their house. Imagine how much of a mess that would be!

"Of course, of course," she agreed awkwardly.

"But you were saying something before," Roberto broke in. "What's going on?"

I took a deep breath and looked at my mom again. She nodded encouragingly.

"Oh, I . . ." I really need a computer for school. Can you help? *Why couldn't I bring myself to say it? "I just wanted to know how you're doing."*

I cringed at my own cowardice.

My mom pursed her lips. Want me to ask? *she mouthed. I nodded, and she dropped the papers she was holding and came up beside me.*

I waited for Roberto to finish talking.

"That sounds great, Dad. I'm going to put Mom on, she wants to talk to you."

My eyes filled with tears as I handed her the phone.

Why was it so hard to ask my own father for the things I needed? Why did he have to go and leave us behind?

Chapter 21

Because I was grounded, I wasn't able to see Diana for the rest of the week.

But she texted me back the day after the Big Reveal, right as I was getting to work.

My mom and I had another fight when I got home

And I forgot to text you and ask if everything was ok

Sorry about that

No worries, you've had a lot on your mind

It's totally understandable

So how did it go?

Was everything ok?

I didn't want to dump my problems on her, so I just said:

> It's under control

> Are you free later?

> Hmm

> There's a slight chance I'm grounded and have a curfew until this weekend . . .

She sent a confused emoji.

> Didn't you say things were under control?

> Yeah, under my dad's control

> Dayana!!

I sent a shrugging emoji.

We texted back and forth for the next few days. I was glad we'd finally gotten past the whole not-talking thing, but I noticed that Diana almost never mentioned the Royal Scandal, as she called it. When she needed to vent, we talked on the phone, as if she didn't want to leave a written record. Was this how her life would be from now on?

Constantly trying to keep her secret from getting out?

As soon as Roberto officially ungrounded me on Saturday morning—after a whole speech about how he'd gone easy on me and wouldn't be so lenient next time, which wasn't at all intimidating because he faltered halfway through, unable to keep up the strict dad act—I texted Diana and asked her to meet me at the Chalk Farm station at three that afternoon.

Since I hadn't been able to go out, I'd spent the past few days planning our next date. I'd had a lot of ideas—the London Eye, a cool restaurant, pedal boating on the lake—but in the end I'd settled for a good old-fashioned picnic. Every Friday, I got my weekly salary: a stack of crisp, clean bills that were just begging to be spent. But I knew that if I wanted to save for my future independence, I'd have to rein myself in. Anyway, I'd already spent too much on our previous dates. So I took advantage of my employee discount to buy a few things for the picnic, then rolled up the rest of the money with a rubber band and put it in my sock drawer.

After lunch, as I was getting ready, Georgia came to my room and flopped down on the bed. Apparently, this was becoming a habit.

"Are you going out with your princess?" she asked, and I froze.

Our eyes met, and I had to bite my lip to keep from laughing.

"You're the worst," I moaned, tossing a dress at her.

She caught it. "Not this one. What about that button skirt you got at Primark?"

"We're having a picnic, so I don't think it'd be comfortable."

She thought for a minute. "Then what about your black romper? The one that looks like a dress?"

I snapped my fingers. "Great idea!"

I rummaged through the wardrobe, which was almost full now. I still hadn't had the heart to fully unpack, and my suitcases lay open on the floor. But as I'd settled in, things had started migrating to the wardrobe after I'd used them. Clothes, makeup, beauty and hygiene products. Now that I looked at them, the suitcases were practically empty.

"I'm so jealous," Georgia joked as I pulled out the romper. "You got here a month ago and you already have a girlfriend."

I looked at her. She pouted.

"Want me to ask if Diana has any friends to introduce you to? Wait—any preferences I should know about?

She mulled this over. "I like tall people, but not if they're too skinny. Gender doesn't matter. As long as they're wearing a crown."

I rolled my eyes.

"You're a real social climber, I see." But the traces of a smile still played around my lips. *Gender doesn't matter* was quite the confession.

"There's no point having a sister who's dating a princess if she doesn't introduce you to an eligible young royal."

I stuck out my tongue at her. "Is that the only reason you like me?"

"I guess you're kind of cool. But only a little." She winked.

I turned toward her, wearing my black spaghetti-strap romper with a white half-sleeve crop top underneath.

"So, how do I look?"

She nodded and gave me a thumbs-up. "Perfect."

I grinned and started throwing things into my bag.

Someone knocked at the door.

"Georgia, amor, are you in there?" It was Lauren.

"Yeah, I'm here!" Georgia yelled.

Lauren opened the door and Ruffles burst into the room, chasing his own tail in crazed circles. She looked at Georgia, who was still on the bed, and then at me.

"Are you going out, querida?" She sat on the edge of the bed.

I shrank back. "I thought I wasn't grounded anymore. I can go, right?"

"Claro, claro! You're free to go," she said quickly. "I was just asking. Do you have a date with your girlfriend?" She gave me a little smile.

My cheeks flushed.

Georgia sat up suddenly, then winced with pain.

"You told her?" she asked me indignantly.

Lauren straightened up, visibly offended. "And why wouldn't she? You know, some people trust me, querida."

"I trust you," Georgia said defensively. She shrugged and looked at her feet. "I just don't have anything to tell."

"Well, maybe you should. Your sister is getting out and enjoying life, and you're stuck here em casa."

It was the first time Lauren had called me Georgia's sister, and a warm feeling spread through my chest.

Georgia scowled. "It's hard to enjoy life when I'm in pain *all the time.*"

Lauren sighed. "I know, amor, but you have to make an effort. You can't just wait around watching life pass you by. You have to try harder."

This was definitely the wrong thing to say, because Georgia stiffened with anger. I rushed to throw a few more things in my bag, snatched my sneakers from the wardrobe and my phone from the bedside table, and grabbed the cooler bag I'd set aside earlier for our picnic snacks.

"I'm going! Bye!"

"Don't get home too late!" Lauren called as I left the room. "And don't ignore our texts!"

"I need to *try harder?*" I heard Georgia ask as I slipped on my shoes in the hallway.

I got out of there before Lauren could respond.

Chapter 22

"Are you saying you told your stepmom about me? I'm *official* now?" Diana brought a hand to her heart. "What an honor!"

I took a sip from my juice box, trying to hide my goofy smile.

We were sitting side by side on a red towel I'd swiped from the hall closet, an array of snacks spread out in front of us: juice boxes; bottled cappuccinos; a carton of every possible kind of berry (including some I'd never seen and didn't know the names of); a box of doughnuts from Rico, the baker at Sugar's Grocery who, when he saw how long I was taking to decide, bugged me until I confessed I had a date, which inspired him to make the order extra special (one of the doughnuts even had little heart-shaped sprinkles on it); and two chicken sandwiches I'd made the night before, after everyone had gone to bed.

Fletcher's "About You" was playing quietly from Diana's phone, part of a playlist she'd put together for the picnic. She'd introduced me to Fletcher a few days before, and now I was obsessed. There was also some One Direction in the playlist, obviously.

"Unfortunately, this isn't the *royal banquet* you deserve, but I think it does the job."

Diana glared at me. I pressed my lips together, trying not to laugh.

"Hilarious."

Maybe Georgia was starting to rub off on me.

"So you and your mom had a talk?" I spread a napkin on my lap and reached for a sandwich. "You said she gave you an ultimatum?"

Diana sighed and popped a blueberry into her mouth. Or was it a cranberry? I couldn't keep any of them straight.

"Sim, we talked."

She looked out at the landscape before us. First, the grassy expanse of Primrose Hill, packed with other couples and families enjoying the clear day. Then a web of crisscrossing tree-lined paths, and finally a row of buildings peeking out behind the leafy green treetops, the bright blue sky arching overhead. It was a breathtaking view.

"She told me a little more about what happened, but it's complicated."

"Which is exactly what I'd expect from a story involving the royal family."

Diana smiled weakly. "She said they met at Universidade de . . . St. Andrews. In Escócia—that's how you say Scotland, right?"

She was struggling to tell the story in Portuguese, so I interrupted her.

"You can speak English, I'll understand," I offered helpfully.

She shook her head.

"I think it's probably safer in Portuguese." She took a deep breath. "One of my mom's friends met Arthur at a pub through another friend, and they ended up in the same social circle. I don't know the details of how they went from amigos to something more, but it doesn't really matter, does it? They liked each other, they hooked up, and that's where I come in." She raised her eyebrows, as if it made her nervous just thinking about it. "And then . . ." I held my breath. The suspense was killing me. "Well, royalty happened."

"Did they threaten your mom?" I asked, still chewing a bite of my sandwich.

"A scholarship student, not to mention a daughter of immigrants, wasn't exactly the kind of wife King Oliver wanted for his grandson."

"Did he meet with your mom and hand over an envelope full of cash so she would go away?"

The thought made her laugh.

"Not in person, anyway. The king would never deal with something like that himself." She waved a hand dismissively, as if she knew all about these things. "But that's more or less what happened."

"But how did the king know she was pregnant if she hadn't even told Arthur?" There were so many layers to this story, it made my head spin.

"I don't think he knew about the pregnancy. He got involved because things were getting serious, to the point where the tabloids were reporting on the prince's girlfriend. Since Andrew had come out of the closet, Arthur was pretty much the king's 'only hope.'" Diana rolled her eyes. "Basically, he stepped in to keep the story from blowing up. My mom liked Arthur, but not enough to get mixed up in all of that. So she took the money, dropped out of school, and went to Brighton."

"Then why did she decide to come back to London?"

Diana shrugged. "She'd gotten a job here, and considering that she'd dropped out of university, it was a really good offer. She'd worked her way up at Sugar's Grocery, and they paid for her to finish her degree. Plus, it had been a long time. She thought it was safe to come back to London."

"But what about the money they gave her?" I felt like I was interrogating Diana, but I couldn't help it. This whole story was *insane.*

"She put it in a savings account for me."

"And why tell the truth now?"

"Because King Oliver died."

I sat there in silence for a while, trying to absorb everything Diana had said. And imagining how hard it all must have been for Rose.

"So Arthur really didn't know about you?"

She shook her head.

"Maybe it was for the best, though. It's not like he refused to meet you or take the paternity test or anything."

"No, not at all. He was very . . . thoughtful. Atencioso, I think?"

Her eyes lit up, and I could imagine how she felt. He sounded like everything I wanted my own father to be.

"It's still really weird. I feel like I'm dreaming, you know? And not necessarily a good dream, either—it just doesn't feel real. I mean, I'm talking to you about the *prince*"—she lowered her voice—"being my dad?! It's like all of a sudden my life is the bloody *Princess Diaries.*"

I smiled at her, and she smiled back. She seemed more relaxed after talking with her mom, as if she was finally starting to accept her new reality. For the first time since we'd met, all the fear in her eyes, all the uncertainty, was starting to disappear. I didn't know if she was ready to be part of the royal family—and as an illegitimate child, she would only ever be halfway in, getting a lot of media attention without being fully accepted by the family—but I could tell she was happy. Happy to know that her dad was alive. That he wanted to be a father to her, even if things weren't as normal as she would have liked.

Diana put her hands in the grass behind her and leaned back to admire the view. She was wearing paper-bag shorts and a light, comfortable button-down. She was always beautiful, but that day she seemed to glow. You know when you're at a fancy mall and everyone is wearing shorts, T-shirts, and flip-flops, but you can tell they cost more than what your mom makes in a year? That was the vibe she was giving off.

In that moment, Diana felt so far from me and my world. Like a princess.

She caught me staring, and the spell broke.

I speared a raspberry on my fork and offered it to her. "I was thinking how well you'd fit into the official family photos."

She burst out laughing and sat up again, brushing off her hands before taking the fork.

"There's one thing I'm curious about, though," I said, nibbling on a berry. She raised her eyebrows. "After everything that happened, why did your mom name you Diana?"

She grinned. "My mom's obsessed with Diana Ross."

I couldn't help laughing. "What? Seriously? So you weren't named after the Queen?"

"No, she really loves Diana Ross. It's kind of annoying how much she listens to her sometimes." Diana laughed a little, then shrugged. "But my mom also said that a few months after she moved to Brighton, the princess called to apologize for everything, including for taking so long to get in touch. She said sometimes the king did things on the DL and she never even found out. And she said if my mom wanted to go back to university in Scotland, she would personally take care of everything. My mom refused the offer and didn't mention that she was pregnant, but I think she's admired the princess ever since. So maybe I was partly named after her, too."

I blinked. I didn't think it was possible to have more respect for the Queen than I already did, but here I was.

"Wow, she's really amazing."

"I know, can you believe she's my *grandma*?"

I straightened up, my eyes wide.

"Oh my god, I hadn't even thought of that!" I flopped onto my back. "I need a minute to process."

Diana giggled and ate a few more berries. Then she picked up her phone and switched to a new song.

"Do you know this one?"

I listened: The musician snapped their fingers, then plucked the first few chords on an acoustic guitar. I shook my head and sat up again.

"It's called 'Best Part' by Daniel Caesar and H.E.R. It reminds me of you. *You're the coffee that I need in the morning. You're my sunshine in the rain when it's pouring,*" she sang in a slightly husky voice.

I smiled at her, touched, as I listened to the rest of the lyrics.

When she lay down with her head in my lap, I ran my

fingers through her hair. The red strands shone between my fingers. Her shirt had slipped off one shoulder, revealing a rainbow tattoo on her collarbone. I traced it with my finger.

"How do you identify?"

"Pan," she said, her eyes closed. "What about you?"

"Bi. For a while I identified as pan, but then I realized bi was a better fit for me. And I like how it sounds." I grinned.

There were a lot of conflicting views about the difference between the two, but over time, I came to understand that bisexuality didn't reinforce the gender binary, as some people said. Either way, the important thing was for everyone to choose whichever term felt right for them. And *bisexual* fit me like a glove.

"It was the same for me, except the other way around. I actually thought I was a lesbian at first. I was always more interested in women, but sometimes I was attracted to people of other genders, so I ended up identifying most with pansexuality."

"Have you dated anyone before?"

"I was seeing this one girl, but it didn't last long. It was more of a . . . what's it called again? A flash in the pan."

I frowned at the English expression. "What do you mean?"

"It's when something is really exciting, but then it's over almost as soon as it starts."

"Oh! We call that fogo de palha. Like, a fire made from straw."

Her hoarse laugh washed over me. "Exactly!"

"I had *a thing* with a boy last year," I said, using the English word because I wasn't sure if she'd understand the Portuguese one. "But it ended when my mom died."

Diana opened her eyes and looked up at me, her head still in my lap. "What was she like?"

"My mom?"

Diana nodded. I looked at the group a few yards below us on the hill, all of them laughing at something. "She was like a shooting star. Bright, strong, impressive. The kind of person who everyone admires."

"Like you," she added, making me smile. "You must miss her a lot."

"So much it hurts."

"I don't know what it's like to lose someone that close to you, but it's sort of like how I felt about my dad. It's strange to miss someone you never knew, though. Like having a hole where other people have flesh and blood."

"For me it's more like someone drilled a hole where there used to be flesh and blood."

She frowned sympathetically and took my hand. I studied the flowers tattooed around her wrist.

"How many tattoos do you have?" I asked, interlacing my fingers with hers.

Her hands were delicate and bony, and there was a freckle on her ring finger.

"Just the two. You actually can't get a tattoo here if you're under eighteen. But my mom took me to Ireland for my sixteenth birthday and got them for me as a gift."

"When's your birthday?"

There were so many things I wanted to ask her. So many things I still didn't know. Basic things, like her favorite color, her favorite ice cream flavor, what superpower she would choose. And deeper things: her greatest dream, where she saw herself in the future, and what she would buy if she had a million pounds.

I wanted to find out where else she had freckles, if there were other constellations on her skin, if holding hands while watching a movie was as nice as I imagined, if sharing a plate of food was actually romantic. If all the things that struck me as cheesy now would be better by her side.

I had so many questions for her. And, just like with my mom, I thought I had all the time in the world.

But then Diana's phone pinged.

And suddenly, it all came crashing down.

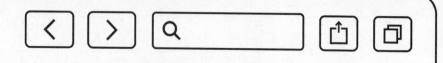

Prince Arthur: The Shocking Truth

Duke of York has illegitimate daughter, sources say

by Chloe Ward

The likely breakup of England's most beloved couple (at least according to rumours) had us all on the edge of our seats. But now we know the truth—and it's beyond anything we could have imagined.

A trusted source has revealed that the mysterious woman seen recently with the prince is none other than a past lover. And most shocking of all: the mother of his child.

It seems Arthur met Rosane Lima, the daughter of Brazilian immigrants, at university in 2004. The resulting summer fling produced a child, though Arthur had no knowledge of her until a few weeks ago.

Apparently, the same is true of his teenage daughter.

Lima hid life-changing information from both father and daughter: the existence of his firstborn child and the truth of her parentage.

The only question that remains is why.

* * *

For more up-to-the-minute news about the scandal of the decade (or maybe the century), subscribe to our newsletter.

Chapter 23

Diana stared at her phone, horrified.

"Bloody bollocks bastard!" she burst out. In my mind, I translated it to the Portuguese equivalent of "Goodness gracious me!" which felt more appropriate for a princess.

I leaned toward her. "What's up?"

She handed me the phone, and a second later, my horrified expression matched hers. The first thing that caught my eye, even before the headline, was the photo of Diana and Rose right below it. It was a paparazzi photo, so the quality wasn't great, and they weren't that close to the camera. But it was definitely them.

"Holy shit," I murmured. I looked at Diana, stunned. "But . . . how?"

"I don't know!" she said shrilly.

She took her phone back and called someone.

"What happened? How did this get out?" she asked in English as soon as the person picked up. I guessed it was Rose. "No, I don't know! I have no idea who could have leaked it. No, I didn't . . ." She glanced up at me. "I didn't tell anyone."

Her voice bordered on panic. She brought a hand to her mouth and started chewing her thumbnail, then finally said, "Just stay calm. I'll take a cab home. Be there soon."

She hung up and looked at me, devastated. I rushed to gather our things, stuffing food haphazardly into the cooler bag.

"Don't worry, it'll all work out," I said as I packed up. "It's a bad photo—no one will be able to tell it's you. And the royals are experts at sweeping things under the rug."

"Day . . ." she said weakly. "You didn't . . . you didn't tell anyone, did you?"

I froze with the carton of berries in my hand.

"I'm not accusing you," she said quickly. But she was. "It's just . . . everyone at the palace who *knew* signed a non-disclosure agreement. If they told anyone, they'll have to pay a really big fine. And other than them, I only told you. I don't know, is there any chance you let something slip or . . . could someone have overheard us?"

I still couldn't move.

My worst fears were coming true. I'd told Georgia, and the story had leaked to the press. Soon it would be in all the newspapers and magazines. But Georgia wouldn't have told anyone . . . would she? I trusted her.

Except Diana had also trusted me. And I'd spilled her secret.

Was *I* the one who'd screwed up?

"Day, you didn't tell anyone, right?" Diana asked again, more sharply this time.

I gulped.

"Just my sister," I whispered. Her eyes bulged.

"Day!" She jumped to her feet, and a few people looked over at us. "I can't believe it! I trusted you."

I stood up, too.

"I know, but I didn't mean any harm, I swear," I pleaded. I took her hands, trying to get her to look at me. "She knew about my suspicions and wouldn't stop bugging me. But it couldn't have been her, Diana. Why would she do something like that?"

"*Money*, maybe?" she hissed, her face livid. "Attention? So she could tell people her *sister*"—she made air quotes with her fingers—"was going out with the prince's bastard daughter? God, I was such an idiot! I should've known when I saw you at the palace. But instead I told you the truth and you went and shouted it to the whole world!"

I stepped back, dropping her hands, and shoved the rest of my stuff into the cooler bag.

"So now that you're a princess, you think everyone's a backstabber who'll do anything for fifteen minutes of fame?" I had the decency to keep my voice down. "I never thought someone could change so quickly."

I turned on my heel and headed toward the park entrance.

"Why are you so offended?" She was following me. "I thought you hated everyone in that house."

I spun around so abruptly, she almost bumped into me. "You think I would tell your secret to someone I hate? Is that the kind of person you think I am?"

She seemed startled. "Of course not, I—"

"It's fine, I know I messed up," I interrupted. An anger I'd never felt before, not even in my arguments with Roberto, seemed to have invaded every cell in my body. "I'm sorry, I really am. I promised not to tell anyone, and I broke that promise. But you didn't hesitate for a second before accusing me and my sister, even though everyone at the palace loves gossiping and talking anonymously to the press. So you know what? Maybe it's time to accept your new reality and start hanging around with people like you. That way you won't have to worry about backstabbers like me anymore."

And I strode off toward the Underground, mad as hell.

By the time I got home, my anger had turned into frustration, and my frustration into tears. I tried to slip into my room, but Lauren's eagle eyes spotted me, and before I even reached the bed, she was opening the door.

"What happened, querida?" she asked, her voice full of concern. I dropped my bags on the floor and threw myself on the bed without a word. "Did you have a fight with your girlfriend?"

Just hearing the word *girlfriend* made my stomach hurt.

I'd ruined everything. I'd destroyed the best thing that had happened to me since my mom died. And it was all my fault. *Again.*

"Leave me alone, Lauren!" I shouted, pulling my pillow over my head as if it could protect me from the world.

I wanted to close my eyes and rewind my life. Go back to that day six months before and do everything differently. Save my mom. Hug her tight. Never let her out of my sight again.

The mattress sank as Lauren sat down next to me. She didn't say anything, but she stayed there for a few minutes, rubbing my back while I sobbed. Then the door opened again.

"Day, what happened?" It was Georgia.

I jumped up, startling Lauren, and stared Georgia down.

I don't know what came over me. I'd defended her to Diana, and I knew she didn't have any reason to tell anyone, but for some reason my mind flew back to what she'd said earlier about being jealous of me.

"Did you tell someone?" I asked accusingly.

"Dayana, amor, calm down—" Lauren began.

"What?" It took Georgia a second to catch my meaning. Then a guilty look crossed her face, and I knew. I *knew.* "I . . . I . . ." she stammered.

"Oh my god, it was you! You told. You actually *told*!"

Diana's accusations came back to me, and I felt like the worst person in the world. Because now I knew exactly how she felt. And it was *awful.*

"Were you jealous? Were you mad at me?" I thought these were more likely explanations than money or fame. "You did a good job pretending you liked me, but I know you don't want me here. I know I came and messed everything up and you were all much happier without me."

"Stop that, amor." Lauren patted my leg reassuringly. "We love having you here."

"Don't lie to me!" I yelled, pushing her hand away.

"Don't talk to my mom like that!" Georgia yanked on my arm. "It's time for you to wake up and stop being such a spoiled little brat! Yeah, you got here and messed things up, but we still did our best to make you feel at home. Maybe if you'd realized how lucky you are, none of this would have happened!"

"Oh, so now it's my fault you're such a gossip?"

"You know what, if you don't like it here, you can just GO BACK TO BRAZIL!"

"Get out of my room!" I screeched so loudly it hurt my ears. She didn't need telling twice.

Lauren sat there looking lost. She clearly had no idea what was going on. But in the end, she followed Georgia out of the room. When she shut the door, leaving me alone with my guilt, I collapsed on the floor. And I cried like I hadn't cried since that terrible day, six months earlier.

I couldn't stop crying.

The tears ran down my face as I dialed my mom's number.

"Hi, Lady Day! I was just thinking of you—" she started, without letting me get a word in. I sniffled, and she broke off. "Is everything okay?"

"Mom . . ." My voice was shaking. I knew it would worry her, but I couldn't help it. "Can you come get me?"

A noise on the other end told me she'd dropped whatever she was holding. I heard the tinkling of keys.

"Where are you? What happened?"

"I'll text you my location."

"Weren't you going to the movies with Heitor?" The car chirped as she unlocked it.

"Yeah, but the movie we wanted to see was sold out, so we went to get fries at Marechal and . . ." Thinking about it made me start crying again. "Just come get me, Mom."

I was too ashamed to tell her what had really happened.

Heitor and I were eating our fries when some of his friends happened to walk by. And then . . .

"Heitor?!" they yelled, startling us.

I watched it all happen: His eyes widened, and he looked from his friends to me. And then he stood up so suddenly his chair fell over.

I'd seen all three of them before—they were his crew

from school. Two boys who were so tall, pale, and skinny that they reminded me of praying mantises, and one who was short and fat. They came up to our table.

"What are you doing here, man?" asked one of the praying mantises, eyeing me curiously.

They didn't even say hi to me. It was like I was invisible.

I felt myself shrink into my seat.

"Nothing," Heitor said, too quickly. "This was the only open seat, so I asked if I could sit here."

He tapped the table.

"Thanks again," he said simply. Then he walked off with his friends.

Shame hit me like a tsunami. I turned in my chair, wanting to rip him a new one, but when I opened my mouth, nothing came out.

Before they disappeared from view, I heard one of his friends say, "Damn, dude, you scared me. For a second there I thought you were on a date with chubby over there."

To which Heitor responded, laughing, "Are you crazy, man? She's not my type at all. She looks like Miss Piggy."

It was like a dam had burst and an entire river of tears was pouring down my face. Emi and Lara were right. They'd been right the whole time. I'd just refused to see it. I felt like a piece of trash, worse than a pile of dog shit.

I cried so much that one of the employees came to ask if I was okay.

When I'd calmed down a little, I called my mom. And then the tears came back.

"Don't worry, I'm on the way!" my mom said desperately. "Wait for me in a store or a restaurant, okay?"

"Okay."

She hung up, and I sat there in the same spot, near the famous Marechal french fry stand, eating the rest of our fries by myself. I don't even like them that much, *I thought angrily, throwing one back down on the plate.*

As night fell with no sign of my mom, I started to get worried. I called her again and again, until someone finally picked up.

But it wasn't her.

Chapter 24

Diana hadn't reached out to me since our fight, and things at home were even worse than they'd been the day I arrived. Going to work was a huge relief, except when I ran into Rose. This didn't happen often, though—because of the Royal Scandal, she spent more time out of the office than in it.

People on the street now recognized her as Prince Arthur's old flame, and, unsurprisingly, the employees at Sugar's Grocery couldn't stop talking about it. I left the stockroom as little as possible, because every new comment pushed me deeper into despair. I wanted to text Diana and ask how she was dealing with all the publicity, but I couldn't bring myself to do it. Guilt and resentment snowballed inside me, and with every day that passed, I felt more and more frustrated with myself and with the world.

I was a ticking time bomb.

Georgia and I weren't on speaking terms, either. I was angry, but I also felt bad. Her pain had gotten worse since our argument.

As I left work the following Friday, I could feel the guilt weighing on my shoulders.

The last thing I expected was to find my dad's silver Ford Focus waiting for me outside.

I didn't really believe it was him until the window rolled down and Roberto leaned over the passenger seat.

"I came to get you," he said. *Thanks, Captain Obvious.*

"Why?" I asked. But I still got in the car, slamming the door a little harder than necessary before putting on my seat belt.

He ignored the question.

"So, how was work?" He seemed relaxed, but I still hadn't forgiven him for our last fight.

"Fine," I said flatly.

"Lauren and I are looking for an English tutor for you. We're hoping to find someone who can start in July. That way you'll feel ready for school in the fall," he went on, in the same cheerful tone as always.

I sat there in silence, staring out the window. I hadn't spent much time in cars here, so I still wasn't used to the fact that the English drive on the left. It freaked me out every time Roberto turned the "wrong" way, especially when there was another car coming.

"I know the accent here is hard at first," he said. Maybe it was just me, but I thought he hesitated for a second, as if forcing himself to keep up the conversation. "But soon you'll understand everything without even trying. Especially now that you're working. You're young, and you're smart as a whip."

"Mhm."

"I never made much of an effort to learn, even though I've lived here for so long." He shifted in his seat and flicked on his blinker. I steeled myself for the turn. "You get comfortable, you know? Other Brazilians help you find work, and the employers don't really care if you speak English as long as you get the job done. Time flies, and you don't even realize it. But in the end I learned enough to get by."

"You . . ." I stopped myself. Roberto turned to me, startled, then quickly looked back at the road. I almost regretted speaking up, but curiosity got the better of me. "You weren't scared? Of coming to a different country all by yourself?"

What had it been like for him to move across the Atlantic to a place where he didn't speak the language or know anyone who could help him if he needed it? I had much more support than Roberto did when he moved here, and it was still scary. He must have been shitting his pants.

"Of course I was! But I was also scared of staying in Brazil." He looked at me from the corner of his eye. Was he trying to figure out how honest to be with me? "A serious recession hit Brazil, and I was laid off the next year. No one

235

was hiring—at every single business it was cut, cut, cut. Luckily, I'd worked at OdontoCorp long enough to get a decent severance package. And then I heard about one of Aunt Mara's friends. He'd moved to England a year earlier and was doing really well. Even though the crisis had affected Europe, too, there was still work for immigrants. They were cutting official jobs, not informal work. Anyway, I had to decide quickly, because otherwise the whole severance package would be eaten up by . . . our costs." He paused and cleared his throat. By *costs*, he meant my mom and me. "So I took the risk. And . . . well . . ." He held up his hands, as if to say *Here we are.*

And was it worth it? I thought, tears welling in my eyes. *Was it worth giving up everything for* this?

Instead of saying it out loud, I swallowed the lump in my throat and asked, "Why did you come get me?"

He seemed taken aback by the sudden change of topic.

"I, uh . . . Lauren and I were thinking of taking you two out for dinner." He cleared his throat again. "We could all use some family time."

Aha. They were trying to broker some sort of peace between Georgia and me.

I crossed my arms, anxious at the thought of seeing her again. Roberto slowed down and pulled into a parking spot.

He led me to a fifties-style diner where the waitresses

were dressed like pinup girls and the waiters had hair like Elvis, and they all rolled around on roller skates. There was a jukebox up against one wall, and the booths had red leather seats and aluminum accents, like the inside of an old car.

Under normal circumstances, I would have loved it.

And it would have been the perfect place to take Diana. I'd find out how she liked her hamburgers, and whether she preferred milkshakes or soda with her fries (or maybe juice? Now that I thought of it, I'd never seen her drink soda). We'd pick songs for each other on the jukebox.

I pushed the thought away before I got even more depressed.

Lauren and Georgia were already there, in one of the booths at the back. Georgia was typing on her phone and didn't even look up when I arrived. I crossed my arms and ignored her right back.

A blond Elvis came to take our order, and I reluctantly handed over my menu, wishing I could make a little tent with it and crawl inside.

He went back to the counter, and we sat there in silence for a few seconds.

Then Lauren raised the worst possible subject:

"It's absolutamente outrageous! A secret sixteen-year-old daughter." She was talking about the Royal Scandal, oblivious to my discomfort. Apparently, Georgia hadn't explained why we were fighting. She was probably embarrassed by how badly she'd messed up.

She peeked up through her eyelashes, her head still lowered.

"He must have known, right?" Lauren snapped her fingers. "Oh! I bet they paid her to disappear."

I closed my eyes and took a deep breath, trying to contain my annoyance. After the miserable week I'd had, Lauriane's voice had started to grate on my nerves again.

Our hamburgers took forever to arrive, but when Blond Elvis finally rolled up with the tray, I almost kissed him out of sheer relief. The food would give us a few moments of peace.

"Georgia," Roberto said suddenly, after we'd been eating for a while. He and Lauren exchanged what I thought was a meaningful glance. Georgia looked up coldly. "Have you made any progress on finding an English tutor? Are any of your classmates interested?"

"No. No one's responded yet. They may be on holiday."

She turned her attention back to her burger, which was strangely untouched.

"Oh, right." He fell silent, and I caught Lauren staring at him sternly. "Uh, is there any way we can get in touch with them more quickly?"

She shrugged.

"Maybe—" he started to say, but then Georgia jumped to her feet.

"I'm going to the bathroom," she said, her face contorted with pain. I felt an urge to ask if she needed help.

But I didn't.

And the next second, she stepped out of the booth and fainted.

Chapter 25

Fibromyalgia.

That's what the emergency room doctor thought she had.

It made sense. The most common symptoms were pain and tenderness throughout the body, and no one knew what caused it. I'd only heard of it because it was the reason Lady Gaga canceled her Rock in Rio show. But I'd never done any research on it or known anyone who had it.

Until then.

"Why didn't you tell anyone how bad the pain was?" I asked Georgia the next day.

She'd spent the night hooked up to an IV in the hospital because she couldn't even bring herself to eat. When she came home that morning, she only made it up to her room because they'd given her a bunch of painkillers.

Georgia had been an asshole to me, but I didn't want her to be *sick*. She was curled up in bed with her face to the wall. I sat in her desk chair, feeling terrible. We'd been fighting, but still, I should have noticed something was wrong.

"I *did* tell you. You thought I was exaggerating," she said bitterly.

I tried to think of something to say. She was right, of course. We'd believed her, but we'd all underestimated the amount of pain she was in.

Georgia hadn't reacted well to the fibromyalgia theory, mainly because there was no cure. She'd cried nonstop, even though the doctor kept saying he didn't know for sure yet. Deep down, she must have known it was the most likely diagnosis.

She'd have to take a bunch of tests to rule out other illnesses first. Apparently, there still wasn't a way to test for fibromyalgia. But if the diagnosis was confirmed, the doctor could suggest some strategies to minimize her symptoms, including physical activity, pain medication, and potential psychiatric support.

"Just leave me alone, Dayana," Georgia said after a while. "I want to be by myself."

"And why should I do what you say?" I asked, playing with the lever below my seat. The chair sank all the way down. "After all, I'm only your fake sister."

She turned to me, trying to look annoyed. But her grimace of pain ruined the effect.

"Can you stop? I don't want to talk to you. Just go away."

I hung my head.

"Sorry," I whispered, even though she was the one who'd screwed me over.

I left before I could make things worse.

I closed her door carefully and sighed, leaning back against the wood. I wanted so badly to erase the last few days and go back to how things had been before Saturday. I wanted to forget that Georgia had betrayed my trust, that *I'd* betrayed Diana's trust, that everything was an absolute train wreck.

I was on my way down the stairs when Lauriane's voice stopped me.

"What will we do if they confirm the diagnosis, amor? I can't bear seeing her like this. Não aguento." The bedroom door muffled her voice, but I could tell she was exhausted. "I wish I'd tried harder to figure out what the problem was. She must be in so much pain!"

"Stop that, honey. It's not your fault." But Roberto sounded equally worried. "Neither of us had ever heard of it, and none of the other doctors told us about it. How were we sup-posed to know? But we'll figure it out. We always do, right?" As encouraging as this little pep talk was, I sensed he was fighting a losing battle against hopelessness.

"I disagree, Roberto. I don't think I kept a close enough eye on her. I should have paid more attention." I could hear her pacing back and forth. "And after Dayana got here . . . well, the crisis got worse. I knew that, but I didn't want to admit it. All that stress can't have been good for Georgia's health."

My heart lurched. Lauren was blaming *me*?

"What do you want me to do, Lauren?" my dad asked, a hint of irritation in his voice. "I know it hasn't been easy dealing with Dayana, but she's having a hard time, too. It's not like I could have turned her away. She's my daughter."

I almost smiled when I heard that. Except I was still too stunned.

Lauren scoffed. "Of course not. Dayana needed us, and we would never have turned her away. It was just bad timing. Right when Georgia got sick, Dayana arrived. She had those temper tantrums, and Georgia's pain got worse. It was just too much. Demais. I'm so tired." Lauren's voice broke, as if she was on the verge of tears.

"I know, honey, but we'll work something out. Don't worry," said Roberto, more calmly now.

I heard footsteps in the bedroom, and then silence.

Before they could come out and catch me eavesdropping, I tiptoed down the stairs as quietly as I could, which wasn't saying much, because every floorboard in that godforsaken house creaked like crazy.

But they were clearly too concerned with the family I wasn't part of to remember that I lived there, too. To be discreet when they talked about me.

Or maybe they just didn't care. Because, after all, hadn't I left everyone exhausted?

I should've been happy that their whole perfect family act had fallen apart before I could get too attached. They were starting to worm their way into my feelings, slowly putting me at ease. Pretty soon I would've felt at home.

But I wasn't.

That house wasn't a home.

In a real home, you weren't accused of making your fake sister sick.

In a real home, you were accepted, not out of pity but because they wanted you there.

In a real home, you were loved.

That house wasn't a home.

I'd always known that, but sometimes it was easier to accept an illusion than reality. It wasn't hard to get used to it when I didn't have anything else.

The tears spilled down my cheeks before I could stop them, and something splintered inside me. All I wanted was to call Diana and run into her arms. But I didn't have that anymore. The whole life I'd built so carefully in that distant place had shattered, as if it was made of porcelain.

This house, this city, this entire country—suddenly all of it was suffocating me.

But what could I do? Run away?

It was like a light bulb went on in my head.

I was in free fall.

Every hour.

Every minute.

My world was in pieces.

My mom was dead.

Because of me.

The thought coiled like a snake inside me.

Terrifying.

Suffocating.

Poisonous.

And I was falling, defenseless against its deadly bite.

Chapter 26

The seat belt sign came on with a ping, waking me from an unsettling dream.

"Attention, crew members. Prepare for landing," the pilot announced over the loudspeaker.

The plane jolted as we lost altitude, making my stomach drop. I shifted uncomfortably in the middle seat. Unfortunately, buying a last-minute ticket meant I couldn't get an aisle seat, so I'd had to hold in my pee for hours. I'd been so emotionally exhausted that I'd spent more than half the flight sleeping, and the rest of the time I'd watched sad movies so I could cry without getting side-eye from my neighbors. It was only when the screen in front of me lit up with instructions for landing that it dawned on me what I'd done.

Holy shit.

I was going back to Brazil.

I'd waited for everyone to go to bed before taking the emergency credit card from the living room drawer and booking a seat on the next flight to Brazil. I'd packed a suitcase with the things I needed most—I couldn't bring *everything* because I'd bought the cheapest ticket, and anyway, more luggage meant I was more likely to wake someone. I'd called an Uber right before sunrise, also with the emergency credit card, and snuck out as quietly as I could.

Yeah, I knew how irresponsible this was—much worse than lying about going to work and then disappearing for a few hours—but it felt like my only choice. I honestly couldn't stay in that country for another second. I'd taped a note for Roberto and Lauren to my door, apologizing for messing up their life and using their credit card and promising I'd pay them back (I wasn't sure how, given the current exchange rate, but I'd figure something out). I'd also left behind the weight on my chest, which had been threatening to crush me.

The lights of Rio de Janeiro twinkled outside, and I felt a rush of emotion at the nighttime view of *my* city. When the plane thudded down on the runway, the adrenaline boost almost brought me to tears again. I stood up to get my bag even before we'd parked at the gate. All I wanted was to get home, hug my grandparents, and spend the rest of the week curled up in bed, trying to forget all the people I'd disappointed.

I knew it wouldn't be easy, especially because I was about to see the disappointment on their faces, too. But as long as they were with me, I'd get through it. I'd forgive them for sending me off without a second thought—unless they tried to make me go back.

The thought made me so anxious that I'd bitten my fingernails down to nothing by the time I rang their doorbell. I still had a key, but I thought they'd be less startled to see me on the doorstep than wandering around the apartment like a ghost. Though nothing could really have prepared them to open the door and come face-to-face with the granddaughter they'd shipped off to England.

And nothing could have prepared *me* to see my grandparents in person again, after an entire month of ups and downs.

"Dayana?" my grandma asked. She frowned and adjusted her glasses, as if she was seeing a mirage. Then she looked over her shoulder. "Tião! Tião!" she called, her voice rising an octave.

When my grandpa came up behind her, just as shocked as she was, I dropped my bags on the floor, wrapped both of them in a bear hug, and burst into tears.

* * *

The next day, I woke up feeling like I'd been run through a meat grinder. I kept my eyes closed, afraid that I'd dreamed the whole thing, that I hadn't really had the courage to go back to Brazil. But the smell of my grandma's fabric softener filled my nostrils, and the rattle of the buses outside, so loud they might as well have driven into the apartment, assaulted my ears. Obnoxious drivers leaned on their horns, and a car with a loudspeaker passed by, announcing, "We'll buy your old fridges, ACs, and stoves!" I was so relieved I almost laughed. It was safe to get out of bed.

I rubbed my eyes, which were swollen from crying, and slowly opened them. Above me was the white ceiling I knew so well, the wooden fan at its center. I smiled and turned over, thinking I might be able to get back to sleep.

That was when I came face-to-face with Emi and Lara.

I sat bolt upright in bed.

"What are you doing here?" I asked, bewildered.

Emi responded by slapping my leg. Hard.

"You. Ungrateful. Asshole." She kept slapping me, visibly angry. Emi had big eyes, but when she got mad, they narrowed so much you could barely see her dark irises. "After all these years of friendship, how could you leave without telling me? *How could you ignore us like that, like we didn't even exist?* I'm really upset with you, Dayana Maria. Really upset." Despite what she'd just said, she threw her arms around my neck and hugged me.

Lara stayed standing, her arms crossed. Her hair was in a bun on top of her head, as if she was about to fight someone.

"You know what pissed me off the most?" she asked, scowling. "You didn't post a single photo on Insta. We couldn't even hate you—we just wanted to know if you were okay! I had to call your grandparents to find out what was going on with you."

Even though they were ganging up on me, I was glad they were there. I'd missed my best friends, missed having someone to talk to, someone who was there for me when I needed to vent. Georgia had been that person for a while, but it wasn't the same.

No one knew me like Emi and Lara did.

"What are you doing here, girl?" Emi cut in, not even giving me a second to breathe. "Were you freezing to death over there? No, wait—I bet the Queen banished you!"

The very mention of the Queen made my stomach churn.

I'd texted Diana before I left to apologize for everything, including leaving her mom hanging at the store. But she hadn't responded.

I shook my head, trying to banish the thought of her.

"England sucks," I said. Afraid I might start crying again, I stared down at my lap. "I never want to go back."

"Poor little rich girl didn't like studying abroad, huh?" Lara said sarcastically.

I looked up in time to catch the mocking look on her face.

Then, out of nowhere, I started laughing and crying at the same time.

"I missed you guys so much," I whimpered, hugging Emi again, but harder this time.

Lara joined us, and suddenly we were one big tangle of arms and hair, all three of us crying and holding one another on my bed, in my room, in my country.

"I know just what will make you feel better," Lara said, grinning, as the hug broke up.

I smiled back. Whatever her idea was, I was sure I would love it.

The scent of my grandma's home-cooked breakfast wafted into the room, and a bicycle bell outside announced the bread delivery boy. I could hear my grandma yelling, "Run, Tião! Go get some rolls for the girls!"

My grandpa rushed outside, the door slamming behind him. Birds chirped on the windowsill, their song blending into the bustle of Rio de Janeiro, and it made me happy.

It was so good to be home.

One after another, people came up to hug me, shake my hand, offer their condolences. They all kept saying how sorry they were.

Sorry for what? It was my fault. If anyone was sorry, it was me.

What if I'd listened to my friends, what if I'd ended things with Heitor, what if I hadn't agreed to get fries with him at Marechal?

So many what-ifs.

The only thing I knew for sure was this: My mom had gotten in a car accident on the way to pick me up, after I'd called her in tears.

Everyone said I was being strong, or that I had to be strong to take care of my grandparents. But who was going to take care of me?

As if trying to answer my unspoken question, Emi came up beside me and put a hand on my back.

"Everything okay?"

I nodded mechanically.

One of my mom's friends came into the chapel and walked up to me.

"She was so young! So much life ahead of her," the woman sobbed, as if she were a member of the family. She patted my arm and looked at Emi with a muted smile. "I'm glad you have friends to support you. It's so important at times *like these." She glanced around. "Your boyfriend's not here?"*

I looked at my feet, feeling exposed.

It was like she'd just shouted to the whole chapel that I was there on my own, abandoned by the boy who'd put my mom's life at risk.

"He'll be here soon," Emi answered for me.

The woman left, and I felt Emi's gaze on the back of my neck.

Did she think this was all my fault?

Chapter 27

"What?! You were hooking up with the prince's daughter?!"

Emi propped herself up on the beach blanket and adjusted her sunglasses. Narrowing her eyes against the light, she looked at me as if a second head had sprouted from my neck. Her pale skin was already pink from the time we'd spent in the sun.

"Yeah, but it's over now." I swallowed the lump in my throat and closed my eyes again to avoid meeting her gaze. I dug my hands into the sand, scooping up a fistful of Barra beach. "It all went wrong. London was a giant steaming pile of shit."

"Ew, Dayana!" Lara complained on my other side. Unlike me and Emi, she tanned easily. Her caramel-colored skin had taken on a bronze sheen. "No more poop metaphors. Let's focus. Can you rewind and start from the beginning?"

"Yeah, tell us *everything*, because I didn't even know you liked girls!"

I opened my eyes again, glancing at Emi. Her face was full of anticipation. No sign of judgment.

I pushed myself up to a sitting position.

An unusually big wave broke in the distance, and the wind carried its salty spray all the way to our blanket. It was winter in Brazil, so the sun wasn't too strong, but I'd never liked summer that much. The weather right now was perfect, and going to the beach really had made me feel a little better. It was a typical day in Brazil, a typical day in Rio. Sinking my feet into the sand gave me a sense of stability. As if suddenly the earth was spinning on the right axis again.

It was a Monday in July. The beach wasn't as crowded as it would've been in summer, but because schools were on vacation, it wasn't empty, either. Noon was approaching, and colorful umbrellas stretched out to the horizon, preventing me from seeing the shoreline. A vendor walked by with an aluminum cooler full of iced maté on one shoulder and a bag of cracker packs on the other, shouting, "Get your maté! Nice cold maté!"

Emi and Lara had been trying to tan, but now, in their eagerness to hear my story, they sat up, too.

I sighed.

"I realized I liked girls three years ago, because of . . . Angélica." I peeked at Emi from the corner of my eye. She and Angélica hated each other because of a stupid fight they'd had on student council.

"Angélica?" She made a face.

"In my defense, it was before you both ran for student council president. It was when she first moved here. I kind of fell in love with her, and it made me reconsider my sexuality."

"But why didn't you tell us?" Lara asked, keeping her tone purposely casual, as if she wanted to be very clear that this wasn't an accusation.

"Isn't it obvious? I was too scared."

They opened their mouths to protest, but I already knew what they were going to say.

"I know it doesn't make sense. I know you wouldn't have judged me. But even the thought of telling people made me feel sick."

Emi nodded. She understood better than anyone.

"I can't say I get that," Lara said, "but I'm glad you're telling us now. You know we'd love you no matter what, right?"

I leaned toward her.

"Does that mean you forgive me for leaving without saying goodbye?" I batted my eyelashes at her and smiled sweetly.

She pushed my head away. "Not yet."

I blew her a kiss and straightened up.

The smell of fried shrimp made my mouth water, and another beach vendor walked by, shouting, "Sandwiches for sale!"

I waited until he was gone before starting the story again.

"Anyway, that was that. I realized I was bi because of her, but then the whole thing with Heitor happened, so I decided to keep it to myself."

"Between those two, I'm *definitely* Team Angélica," Emi declared. Coming from her, it meant a lot.

"I know it was a bad idea to hook up with Heitor, okay?" I winced. Talking about him always made my chest ache. For everything he'd put me through. "I'm not *that* clueless."

"Okay, but enough about Heitor," Emi cut in, and I knew she wasn't just saying that because she wanted to get to the gossip. She knew me better than anyone. "Tell us about the princess."

"She's not a princess. As an illegitimate daughter, she doesn't get a title."

"That's not the point, Dayana." Lara crossed her arms.

I sighed. I didn't want to relive my story with Diana, but now that I'd started, Emi and Lara wouldn't leave me alone until they'd heard all the details.

So I told them everything without even pausing for breath, as if I was ripping off a Band-Aid. When I finished, they sat in silence for a while.

"So she blamed you for leaking the secret you promised to keep, and then you just left?" Lara finally asked. "You didn't even text to say sorry? Or ask for a second chance?"

"Of course not." I crossed my arms and scowled. "Anyway, she would've ignored me."

Actually, I *had* texted before I left. But by then it was too late. Diana didn't want anything to do with me.

"But, like, you get that she was probably freaking out about what would happen now that the story was public, right? Plus, you were a huge asshole." As always, Lara expressed herself with surgical precision and wouldn't even go easy on her best friend.

I'd had a lot of time to reflect, and if there was anything I could say for sure, it was that I'd really messed up with Diana. I'd said that I understood her, that I could relate to her and her pain, but I hadn't supported her when she needed me most. I hadn't been strong for her; I hadn't taken her hand and guided her to solid ground. I hadn't been worthy of her trust.

And because I couldn't bear her accusations, I'd simply run away. I hadn't known what else to do.

Maybe that meant I didn't deserve her.

Emi nodded, and for a second I thought she'd read my mind.

"We all pretend we want to be princesses, but imagine what it would be like to spend your whole life as a regular person and then suddenly a ton of journalists show up at your door and publish a story you've barely had a chance to process." Emi wasn't as blunt as Lara, but her voice was equally accusatory. They were both against me. "And then they tell the entire world that you have a father, and he's a prince, when you were always told he was dead."

I looked at them. "But you guys think I was *wrong* to argue with her? I mean, she accused me without a second thought." I was clinging to that stupid excuse with everything I had.

"Not exactly *wrong* . . ." Emi said hesitantly. "But you're impulsive. You blow up when you're angry. And you have a really hard time saying sorry."

"You're being too nice, Emi," Lara interrupted. She turned to me, a flash of annoyance in her eyes, and I braced myself. She never pulled any punches. "You're stubborn, Day. You don't think things through—you just jump in without trying to see the other side. That's why you disappeared after your mom died. You wouldn't even *let* us support you." She ran a hand through her curly hair, tossing it over one shoulder and then the other in a gesture of irritation. "We know you had a lot to deal with, and it wasn't easy. But seriously, we're your best friends. Or we thought we were, you know? And you didn't just stop talking to us—you moved to another country without even telling us!" Tears shone in her eyes, and she wiped them angrily with the back of her hand. "Do you know how hard that was for us? Every day I wanted to get on a plane and come find you. So I could comfort you, or maybe yell at you. I wasn't sure which."

A lump formed in my throat, and I jumped to my feet, too upset to sit still.

"That's why I left!" I was fuming as I snatched up my things. I wanted to run away again, because otherwise I couldn't bear the hole my mom had left in my heart when she died. I felt anxious, inconsolable, like staying there would make the hole grow and grow until it swallowed me up. "I didn't want anyone else's grief! I didn't want to deal with people crying and giving me their condolences. I didn't want people telling me it wasn't my fault."

The last sentence made Lara flinch.

From the corner of my eye, I could see that people nearby were starting to pay attention to our fight. I wanted to shout at them to mind their own damn business, but Lara spoke before I could get even more worked up.

"Why would anyone say it was your fault?" she asked, her brow wrinkled. "It obviously wasn't."

"But it was!" I yelled, glaring at her so fiercely I thought I might set something on fire.

By now the entire beach was watching us. Even a henna artist had stopped to stare. A teenager behind me shouted, "Fight! Fight! Fight!"

I ignored him, keeping my eyes on Lara.

"It was all my fault! If I hadn't gone out with Heitor that day . . . if I hadn't called her after he left . . ." Without warning, a sob forced its way up my throat. I brought a hand to my mouth, unable to keep going.

It didn't matter.

None of it mattered, because I couldn't stand to be there for another second.

I threw on my flip-flops, ignoring the curious looks and rude whistles, and ran toward the bus stop, sand flying up behind me as Emi and Lara called my name.

Texts poured in from Lara, Emi, and all my other friends. The notifications piled up, the number in the red bubble constantly increasing.

But I didn't want to read any of them.

I didn't want to talk to anyone or face the accusation in their words.

That's why I was hiding from everyone, curled up in a corner of my mom's bedroom—which was now my grandparents' room, because they'd had to move in to take care of me. There'd been some back-and-forth, a discussion about the best place: their house or our apartment? At the end of the day, they thought it was best not to put me through another big change.

And I wouldn't have gone. I didn't want to leave my memories of her behind. I didn't think I had the strength. Holding her old nightgown—the one her grandmother had given her, the one she always loaned me when I was sick, saying it was a magic nightgown that could cure anything—I felt something tear inside me. Her clothes still smelled like her, and part of her still lingered in that room. As if any second she would walk in, put her hands on her hips, and say, "Dayana! Didn't I tell you to wait for me?"

But she wouldn't.

She wouldn't walk in.

She was dead.

My mother was dead, and nothing could comfort me.

How could it, if the person who was best at comforting me was her?

Chapter 28

I slipped into the house as quietly as possible. I didn't want my grandparents to see me crying, and I didn't want them to ask me what happened. I just wanted to be left alone.

"Dayana?" my grandma called as I walked through the living room. I didn't answer, and she followed me. "Dayana? Dayana, what's wrong?"

I threw myself on the bed, burying my face in the pillow. My phone was vibrating nonstop in my pocket, but I didn't want to talk to anyone. There was a lump in my throat, and the hole in my heart had become a bottomless pit, sucking me into nothingness. It was like I'd gone back in time to those terrible weeks after my mom's death.

My grandma rubbed my back, and my grandpa came up beside her.

"Dayana, I need you to talk to me. I know things have been hard, but you can't go on like this." She waited, but I just kept crying. "We're really worried about you."

I let out a cruel laugh.

"Sorry for ruining your peace and quiet by coming back

here," I spat, rage emanating from every pore of my body. It wasn't directed at them, exactly—the person I was mad at was me. "I know you were glad to ship me off to London."

"Dayana, that's not true! I've been heartbroken ever since you left. But we knew how hard everything was for you here, especially having to take care of the two of us. When you mentioned going to live with your father . . . we thought it would be good for you to reconnect with him. You'd have a new life ahead of you in London, in a different place, far from the painful memories of Patrícia."

Still lying down, I turned my head toward her.

"It doesn't matter where I am, Grandma," I hissed, "I'm *never* going to forget my mom. Or the fact that she died because of me."

They looked at each other, horrified.

My grandpa knelt beside the bed, stroking my hair the way he used to when I was little, when I'd stay at their house and wake up from a bad dream in the middle of the night.

"Where did you get that crazy idea, buttercup?" he asked gently. "Of course it wasn't your fault."

"Yes it was!" I burst into tears again, overcome by anger and grief. They were spinning inside me like a tornado, ripping up every good feeling I'd had since her death. Soon there'd be nothing left. Nothing. I couldn't breathe, and I realized it didn't matter where I was. These feelings would follow me to Rio, London, wherever. There was no way out.

No way to escape them. The farther away I went, the more lives I would ruin.

"She was coming to get me when . . . w-when the accident happened," I sobbed. "She was worried about me when she died! She didn't know if I was okay; she didn't know I was just embarrassed."

I sobbed harder.

"It wasn't your fault, Day. Nothing that happened was your fault." My grandma hugged me desperately. I closed my eyes and clung to her, trying to anchor myself. "It was an accident that could have happened anytime, whether or not she was picking you up. The person responsible is the driver who ran the red light. Your mom was always careful, you know that. Even if she was worried about you, she was responsible and knew what she was doing. Your mom loved you. She really loved you."

I was so tired. So tired of feeling adrift.

My grandpa patted my cheek, and I opened my eyes.

"We both know how you feel, buttercup. Losing her was the most painful thing that's ever happened to me. Worse than my heart attack. Worse than going to sleep knowing I might not wake up. If only I knew Patrícia would be okay, I could die in peace." He heaved a sigh. "But God has His reasons, and He chose to take her from us. While she was alive, though, your mom gave you all the love in the world, and I know she was so proud to have raised such a brilliant,

266

beautiful daughter with a bright future ahead of her." When I met his eyes, he took my chin in his hand. "I understand why you feel guilty, even though it's not your fault. You have no idea how many times I've thought, *What if I'd visited her that day? What if I hadn't insisted that she get a driver's license, because she never really wanted one? What if I'd been a better father?* But all those what-ifs won't bring her back."

He pressed his lips together. This was the ace up his sleeve, I thought. Because it was true. In the end, all I wanted was to bring her back.

"The best way to get rid of that guilt is to live fully," he continued. "To treat every day as if it might be our last. To be true to our feelings and ourselves. We can cry, but we should also laugh and be happy. Because that's what she would want if she were here, don't you think?"

He looked at me expectantly, and I nodded. His words were like needles, sewing up the hole in my chest: Yes, they were sharp and painful, but they still worked their magic, stitching the scraps of my heart back together. My grandpa started stroking my head again, the rhythmic motion warming me, soothing me.

My eyes were heavy, and at some point I fell asleep. I dreamed of my mom.

* * *

I was still in bed, but something was wrong. There was a strange shimmer in the air, the way dreams look in movies, and my body felt unbearably heavy, like it was made of lead.

There was a huge digital clock on the wall across from my bed. The pixelated green numbers announced the time: 3:33.

When I was a kid, I had a sleepover with some friends from school. Before going to bed, we told each other ghost stories. According to one girl, 3:33 was the time when demons and ghosts crossed over from the spirit world to our world, and anyone who woke up at that moment would be cursed forever.

Obviously this story had me peeing my pants. Even after the sleepover, waking up in the middle of the night made me so tense I couldn't get back to sleep. On one of those nights, my mom woke up to go to the bathroom and found me in the fetal position in bed, too scared to even shut my eyes.

"Your friends don't know what they're talking about." Her voice was an echo, a distant memory. But when I looked to the side, there she was. Alive. Smiling. Kneeling by my bed looking exactly how she did before she died. "In fact, 3:33 is when the good spirits come out. They watch over our sleep and protect us. We wake up at that time because there's a lot of energy around us, you know? It's when we're most tuned in to the spirit world. People also say that if someone is thinking or dreaming about you, you're most likely to sense it at 3:33."

"Do you think someone is thinking of me, Mommy?" I remembered my younger self asking. "Do you think it's Daddy?"

"I know your dad thinks about you all the time. But do you know who else it could be?"

"Who?"

"The person who loves you most in this world!"

"You mean God?"

My mom chuckled.

"Yes, Him, too. And me, you silly goose." She tickled me, making me laugh until my fears vanished.

The weight that had pinned my body to the bed suddenly lifted. I squirmed in the sheets, laughing along with her, noticing the faint wrinkles on her young face.

She smiled at me, and her face grew sharper, less dreamlike.

"I'm always thinking of you." Her voice was loud and clear. "Always watching over you and making sure you're happy. That's what matters most." Her touch was as light as a feather. "Never forget that I'm right here," she said, putting a hand over my heart. "I'm always with you."

* * *

When I woke up, my grandparents were still there, sleeping on a makeshift bed on the floor, as if they were afraid to leave me alone. I looked over at my bedside table.

A tear slid down my cheek when I saw that it was 3:33.

And I felt at peace for the first time in ages.

It was her, I was sure of it. My mom was the best person in the world at comforting me—no matter where I was.

I knew I couldn't stay there, huddled in the corner of my mom's room. Even if I felt adrift. Even if the world seemed to be spinning the wrong way, leaving me dazed and disoriented.

I couldn't stay there forever.

So, eventually, I got up.

How long had it been since the funeral? Since the day they lowered her coffin into the ground, into a hole like the one in my heart, and buried her in that dark, lonely place?

Hours? Days? Weeks?

I wasn't sure.

Maybe this would be my life from now on. An endless void. The feeling that nothing was as it should be. Was this how adults felt all the time?

It was scary.

I wanted to stay curled up in that corner forever.

But my back hurt, and there were pins and needles in my legs. The world outside was calling me.

So I took my first step back to life.

Chapter 29

Of all the things I expected to happen now that I was back in Brazil, Roberto's visit wasn't one of them.

But when I opened the apartment door the next day, there he was, in the flesh. No big smile or fake compliments this time. He just stood there awkwardly, hands in his pockets.

"Hi, baby girl," he said finally as I stared at him in confusion.

A feeling I couldn't name unfurled in my chest. It felt like the first time he'd called me *baby girl* since he left ten years earlier.

I cleared my throat, shaking myself from my reverie, and stepped back so he could come in.

My grandparents didn't seem surprised to see him.

"It's been a long time, Roberto." My grandpa held out his hand stiffly.

He'd never forgiven my dad for abandoning my mom.

But my grandma still saw him as her beloved son-in-law.

"You must be exhausted, right, Beto?" she asked attentively. "I'm just heating up dinner. In the meantime, would

271

you like some coffee? Or tea? Isn't tea more common in England?" She let out a little laugh, and my grandpa shot her a sidelong glance.

"Coffee would be great, Sônia. You have no idea how much I've missed your coffee."

"Coming right up!" She hurried to the kitchen, my grandpa in tow, leaving Roberto and me alone.

An uncomfortable silence filled the room.

"Uh . . ." I began, scuffing a foot on the floor. "You can sit if you want."

He sat on the couch, and I took a dining room chair.

"Is Georgia doing better?"

He nodded.

"She and Lauren wanted to come, but she's taking a lot of tests this week, to find out if it's fibromyalgia."

Lauren and Georgia wanted to come? I doubted it. After everything that happened, they probably hated me.

I fidgeted in my seat, remembering the conversation I'd overheard. Roberto seemed to be thinking the same thing.

"You heard me and Lauren talking, didn't you?"

I looked away, pulling at a thread that had come loose from the chair seat. "How did you know?"

"Because of the note you left. 'Sorry I intruded on your perfect family.'" Hearing my own words out loud made me blush. "A bit of an exaggeration, don't you think?"

I took a deep breath, preparing for a surge of anger, but it never came. I was tired. All I had left was a sense of wonder. Like a baby who'd just come into the world—everything was new and different. Unfamiliar.

"I thought I had the right," I said simply.

Roberto nodded.

"I think so, too." He looked at his hands, interlaced in his lap. "I'm so sorry you heard that. I hope you know Lauren doesn't really feel that way. She was just worried about Georgia and ended up saying something she didn't mean."

"I know," I said quietly.

"You *are* welcome in our house. We want you to come back."

I shook my head. "I don't think I can."

"Why not?"

I looked at him, and for the first time, I felt an opening between us. Like we could finally talk about the giant elephant in the room.

"Because I can't forgive you," I admitted, my voice faint. It was so strange to finally say out loud all the things I'd been thinking for the last ten years. "Honestly, I don't even know if you're sorry. You never tried to talk to me about it. You never tried to tell me your side of the story." I hesitated, readying myself for the real confession. "Do you know what it was like to find out we weren't going to England anymore because you'd found a new family? Do you know how it felt when Georgia answered the phone and I heard her calling you *Dad*?" My voice shook a little. "I felt betrayed. Abandoned. And I had been. You didn't keep in touch, and you weren't there to see me grow up. You didn't come visit me a single time. One day I had a father, and the next he was gone." A tear rolled down my cheek, and I bit my lip. "And then when my mom died, my world collapsed. And I remember thinking, *Why her? Why not Roberto?*"

He looked down at his hands, but I caught a glimpse of the tears swimming in his eyes.

"I wanted you two to have a good life," he began, and I held my breath. "I never wanted to leave you behind, your mom knew that. I wanted to get a good job, a nice place for us to live, and earn enough money for you to come join me. But finding work was harder than I expected, and I started to think the problem was me. All the friends I'd made there were succeeding, and I . . . I was falling behind." His voice broke, and he cleared his throat. "I couldn't bring you and your mom, but I didn't want to go back to Brazil like a failure. I just felt so alone. I asked your mom to save money and come meet me as soon as she could, but she started having second thoughts. I didn't blame her. I didn't do much to reassure her, and as time passed, I started calling less and less. I was worried she would hear the fear in my voice. And then one day she called and said you weren't coming anymore. And if I wanted to be part of the family, I'd have to go back to Brazil. After that . . ." Roberto took a deep breath. "I started drinking a lot. I didn't know what to do. I was unemployed, far from home, and with no money to go back. And one day I went out drinking and ended up causing an accident. I had to go to court, and I asked some friends for help. That was how I met Lauren. Her cousin is a lawyer, and he agreed to represent me. Soon after that, she helped me get a stable job. So I decided to stay. I didn't want to go back."

I swallowed, but the saliva stuck in my throat. I felt like someone was squeezing my heart in their fist.

"I . . . I get that things didn't work out between you and my mom," I said, sniffling. "But that's not an excuse for disappearing from my life."

Roberto shook his head.

"I know it isn't. I'm not telling you any of this as an excuse. I just hope you know that I never stopped thinking of you, not for a second. But I was a coward." Tears ran down his cheeks. "I didn't want you and your mom to see what I'd become. I didn't want to be that kind of father. And you were so young, it was hard to talk to you, especially because we didn't have video calls back then. In any case, I wasn't there when you needed me, and the only way I could live with my guilt was by telling myself it was better that way. That you didn't need a dad like me."

He couldn't suppress a sob, and I looked down at my lap, fighting back my own tears. Hearing all this was harder than I'd expected.

"That's why," he continued, "when I married Lauren, I tried to be the best father I could be for Georgia. I think it was my way of compensating." Roberto raised his tearful eyes to me. "I'm not asking you to forgive me. I just don't want you to think you weren't loved. I love you so much, and I never stopped loving you. But I'm also human. I'm not perfect, and when I first became a father, I didn't understand how much my actions could affect the tiny, little person you were back then. At the time, I did what I thought was best. It was only later, with Lauren and Georgia, that I started to see how wrong I'd been. But by then I didn't know how to fix it. Lauren always reminded me to call, and when you asked me for something, she always helped me pick the best possible thing. But I was a coward. Such a coward that, when you came to England, I didn't know how to act. And I'm really sorry about that. It's so painful to think that you didn't feel loved. Because you were, always."

I was crying openly now, and I barely noticed when Roberto came toward me. He knelt and took my hands.

"I understand, I really do," I said, trying to blink back the tears. "But I don't know if I can forgive you. It's not that easy."

"I'm not asking you to forgive me. I just want a chance to be a better father. To give you everything I couldn't give while you were growing up." He put a hand on my cheek. "Will you give me that chance? Will you come back?"

I took a few shuddering breaths as he dried my tears.

Still sniffling, I studied him. He was basically a stranger to me, even though we looked so much alike. I counted the freckles on his cheeks, noticed a few white strands in his dark hair. I examined his brown eyes, moist and full of hope.

Finally, I nodded.

"Okay. I think I can do that."

His face broke into a smile, and it was like seeing myself in a mirror. How could two people look so similar when they'd spent most of their lives apart?

It was still a mystery to me.

A mystery that, for the time being, I wanted to solve— though I reserved the right to change my mind later.

"You know you're not off the hook for using my credit card, right?" he said, a hint of amusement in his voice.

I smiled sheepishly.

"Maybe I should rethink the whole second chance thing."

And he laughed.

Chapter 30

The day after Roberto showed up, I revived my old group thread with Emi and Lara and sent them a message.

> I admit it, I'm really stubborn. big surprise, huh?
> Diana always said so, too . . .

> Anyway, I'm sorry for yelling at you guys and for running away and not valuing our friendship. Everything's been so hard since my mom died, and I keep thinking how if I hadn't let Heitor treat me like crap, if I hadn't been with him that day, if I hadn't asked my mom for help, maybe she'd still be alive. I know it's not my fault, it was an accident, but I can't get the what-ifs out of my head. It's just hard to deal with all these feelings without losing my mind.

> But I want you to know I'll try my best not to take it out on you. And I'm sorry again!

> I'm visiting her now if you want to come

> I love you ♥

I put the phone to sleep and straightened up. Roberto was looking at me.

"Shall we?" he asked, nodding toward the door.

We took the elevator downstairs and then Ubered to the cemetery. I hadn't been back since the funeral—first, because I knew it wasn't where my mom really was, and second, because I hadn't had the nerve. But her grave was a symbol. It was a place where I could cry and talk to her and let out my feelings.

So I thought it was time to pay her a visit.

I'd always been scared of cemeteries—they reminded me of horror movies and ghost stories. And since I'd never lost anyone close to me, I'd never had a reason to visit one, at least until my mom died. But at the funeral I'd been too much of a wreck to form an opinion.

On the day of our visit, as I walked through the rows of headstones toward her grave, everything just seemed sad. Short phrases carved below birth and death dates; withered flowers, and some very fresh ones, placed near the stones; wandering visitors weeping over the loss of their loved ones. It was the saddest place on the planet. And in that melancholy place was my mom.

279

When we stopped in front of her grave, I had to take a deep breath before looking at her smiling photo in its small oval frame.

GOD TOOK HER HOME, IT WAS HIS WILL, BUT IN OUR HEARTS SHE LIVETH STILL, read the generic epitaph. I thought my grandma must have chosen it, but I couldn't really remember. All those days felt blurry and muddled, like a dream that no longer makes sense when you wake up.

Was it really God's will? I'd never know.

Roberto crouched down in front of her grave and said a few quiet words. He closed his eyes, resting his hand on the stone. How strange must it be for him to think that his ex-wife, the woman he'd abandoned, was dead?

After a few seconds, he stood up, wiped his eyes, and put a hand on my shoulder.

"I'll wait for you by the gate."

I watched him walk away before turning back to the headstone.

I stared at it, wondering what to say. Then I took out the little poster I'd decorated the day before and stuck it to the stone with double-sided tape, right above the epitaph my grandma had chosen. I stepped back to read it:

I WILL KEEP YOU, DAY AND NIGHT, HERE UNTIL THE DAY I DIE. I'LL BE LIVING ONE LIFE FOR THE TWO OF US.

It was a line from "Two of Us," the song Louis had written for his mother when she died. I couldn't bring myself to listen to it after everything that happened, but it seemed like a better gift than flowers.

"Much more our vibe now, don't you think, Mom?" I asked softly, wringing my hands. It was so strange to be there, talking to her grave. "You made such a mess when you left. Would you have guessed your ex-husband would come visit you? Well, he did, and now I live with him. Who would've thought?" I leaned back, looking up at the clear blue sky. A pigeon flew by overhead. "It was weird at first. But then I started to feel surprisingly at home there. And you know what? Even Lauriane is cool. I wish you two could have met . . ." I thought about Lauren's fierce temper. "Though maybe you wouldn't have gotten along that well. And there's Georgia, too. Remember how I said I wanted a sister my own age? Now I have one . . ."

I looked at the ground, scratching at the dirt with my black sneakers. It was as silent as the grave. *Literally.*

"And can you believe I went to London? I went to all the places we always wanted to see. I fell in love, too." My heart fluttered. It was the first time I'd said that out loud. "I didn't have a chance to tell you before, but I'm bi, Mom. And Diana, the girl I fell in love with, is amazing. Plus, she's an almost-princess." I laughed weakly and closed my eyes. "Too bad I let her go. Now everyone knows she's the prince's daughter, and I honestly don't know how to get her back. She's probably hanging out with a bunch of aristocrats who are all smarter and funnier than me. Though no one can compete with me when it comes to looks, am I right?" I put a hand on the gravestone, trying to feel something, *anything*. A sign, a response. "I just want to hear your voice, Mom. I just want you to hug me and tell me everything will be okay. And help me figure out what to do." Tears were streaming down my face again. "Why did you have to go like that, without giving me a chance to say all the things I needed to say? That I love you, that you were my biggest role model, that I was so damn proud of you. I really wish I could tell you all that . . ."

The rustling of footsteps on dry leaves made me turn around.

"You know you didn't have to say any of that, right?" Emi asked, coming up beside me. Her straight black hair was woven into a braid that fell over her shoulder. Lara was right behind her. "Your mom always knew. She was always so proud of you. The way she used to look at you . . . I wish my mom looked at me like that."

"She loved you so much, Day," Lara added. "And I bet if she was here, she'd give you a talking-to for blaming yourself for what happened." She put an arm around me, and we leaned against the stone. "If you want her to be proud of you, the best thing you can do is be happy."

"And never ignore us again," Emi added.

"And go get your girlfriend back," Lara said.

Emi nodded emphatically. "Exactly. Getting your girl-friend back would be the cherry on top."

I hugged Lara, the tears coming back all at once.

"I love you both so much. You have no idea how much I missed you . . ."

Emi joined the hug, and the three of us cried together, not just from grief, but from love, too. I was so damn lucky to have them in my life. How had I gone so long without talking to them? And how would I go back to London and leave them behind again?

"We'll video call you all the time," Emi said, when I told them about my decision.

"And you'll keep working and earning money in pounds so you can pay for our plane tickets," Lara added. "Because . . . we have to be there at the end of the year."

Emi and I looked at her. "Why?" we asked in unison.

Lara gave us a mischievous grin. "You guys don't know?"

We shook our heads, and Lara grinned wider. She started tapping at her phone.

Finally, she turned the screen toward us.

"Holy shit!" I blurted as soon as I saw the tweet.

One Direction announces year-end reunion.

Then I started screaming. Straight-up losing it. "Oh my god, oh my god, oh my god!"

Emi and Lara joined in, all three of us jumping for joy in the middle of the cemetery.

283

"I can't believe it, I can't believe it!" Emi squealed.

"Oh my god, I've waited so long for this! I *need* to go to London. Work your magic, Day!"

"And *I* need the two of you there with me. It's gonna be incredible!"

Emi was skipping as we headed toward the exit. "Can you imagine the three of us in London? At the One Direction show? Going to pubs!" Her eyes widened and she grabbed me by the shoulders. "Going to royal balls!"

I rolled my eyes. "Keep dreaming."

But inside, I was thinking, *Is there any chance Diana will forgive me? Could we still have a happy ending?*

I pushed the thought away, because I really doubted that the answer was yes.

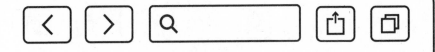

The New Lady Di

Stars Magazine

Diana Rose Lima may not have any claim to the throne or be considered part of the royal family just yet, but she's already being called the New Lady Di.

As beautiful as her namesake, Queen Diana, the sixteen-year-old is on the shy side. But don't let her quiet exterior fool you: Beneath the surface, Diana has a rebellious streak. She's often spotted in a leather jacket, dodging the paparazzi on her trail, and avoiding the media frenzy she's been thrown into. What has most captivated the public, though, is her apparent lack of interest in her royal blood and all the benefits that come with it. Young people all over the world are clamouring for details about the prince's green-eyed, red-haired daughter.

According to Google, "Diana Prince Arthur daughter," "Lady Di young," and "Diana Lima" are among the most-searched terms of the week. After all, don't girls everywhere dream of becoming princesses? Not just because of the crown, the fancy dresses, and the happily ever after, but because they're guaranteed to have the world in the palm of their hand.

Diana Rose Lima hit the jackpot—and she couldn't care less.

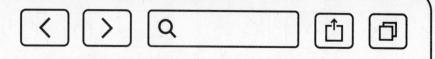

Diana Rose Lima

Diana Rose Lima (Brighton, September 26, 2004) is the firstborn daughter of Arthur Henry Oliver George, Duke of York, and the Brazilian businesswoman Rosane Lima de Oliveira. Until age sixteen, Lima was unaware of her connection to the royal family. In July 2021, an official declaration signed by Queen Diana I confirmed her parentage.

BIRTH AND EDUCATION

Lima was born in Brighton, on the southern coast of England. She studied at White Rose Primary and Secondary School. She will begin her third year of high school in September 2021.

Chapter 31

It was strange to go back voluntarily.

The feeling I had when we touched down in Heathrow was worlds away from what I'd felt the first time. A mix of fear and excitement at the possibilities ahead.

Roberto had come back earlier because he had to work. He'd been able to take some early vacation, but he couldn't spend more than three days in Brazil. After all, he'd have to work a lot to make up for the dent I'd made in his bank account. Last-minute plane tickets weren't cheap, especially when you were buying for two. I should have felt guilty, but he deserved it. It was the least he could do after all those years of not supporting me financially.

I took advantage of being in Brazil to spend as much time as I could with my friends and grandparents, and to enjoy my city as much as possible. I stayed for another week, and on the weekend, my grandparents hosted a barbecue in our building's courtyard. They invited all my old friends and made all the foods I loved, and I had so much fun that I almost decided not to go back to London.

As I walked through Heathrow Airport, the memories of my trip to Brazil felt like a little souvenir stowed away in my heart.

I headed toward Arrivals, where my dad was waiting for me in the car. On the way, though, a bookstore display caught my eye. Among various magazines announcing One Direction's reunion, there was one with a photo of Diana on the cover. My heart sped up. I bought the magazine before going out to meet Roberto.

The royal family had finally made it official, and now the whole world knew her name: Diana Rose Lima, daughter of Prince Arthur, Duke of York.

She wasn't just mine anymore.

* * *

Lauren and Georgia were waiting for me at the front door, the way they had when I first arrived. Ruffles was wagging his tail at their feet. When I got out of the car, he ran up to greet me, barking and leaping with excitement.

"Hey, boy! I missed you so much." I crouched down to scratch his ears as he pranced around me, licking my hands and face.

"I'm so glad you're back, amor!" Lauren opened her arms wide when I stood up, and to my surprise, I hugged her fiercely. "I made you a special lunch." She stepped back and clapped her hands happily. "I called your avós, and they told me you love zucchini lasagna!"

She went back inside, and Roberto dragged my suitcase after her.

Georgia and I stayed behind.

"Hi," she said, sounding embarrassed.

"Hi," I replied, staring down at my feet. "Are you doing better?"

"Yeah, I am. All signs are pointing to fibromyalgia, though."

"Ugh, really? So what happens now?"

"Well, the doctor gave me some meds for when it flares up. But apparently the best treatment is physical exercise, like yoga and Pilates and stuff. And I'm going to see a psychiatrist, too."

"Wow. But it's good that they finally figured out what it is, right?"

"Yeah."

We stood there in silence.

"Georgia—" I started.

"Day . . ." she said at the same time.

We both laughed awkwardly.

Then she said, "I was hoping we could talk. Maybe later tonight?"

"That sounds good. I've been wanting to talk to you, too."

So after dinner, Georgia came to my room, which was exactly how I'd left it.

As soon as she closed the door behind her, she let out a sigh.

"Day, I feel really bad about what I did. I'm so sorry," she said hurriedly, as if she wanted to get it out as fast as possible. She paced back and forth nervously. "When I found out you were coming, I got really stressed. Not because of *you*, but because you being there reminded me of something I didn't have: my own father. Roberto was always a great stepdad, but it's not the same." She ran a hand through her hair. "When I heard you were coming and saw how excited and anxious Roberto was, I had this crazy urge to find my own dad. I wanted to know if he regretted abandoning me, you know? So I started looking for him. My mom had no idea, and I hope she never finds out. But I met him. I met him face-to-face and asked if he regretted it." She stopped pacing and looked at me. "And he said no."

I could see in her eyes how painful that had been. I understood better than anyone.

"Georgia . . ."

Her lower lip trembled. "He said he never wanted to be a father. He asked my mom to get an abortion, but she refused. He thought it was better to leave than be a bad father. Which makes sense, I guess. But hearing him say that . . . hearing him say to my face that he didn't want me to be born . . . it was so horrible."

She started crying, and her legs gave way. Huddled on the floor, she sobbed quietly. I went over and patted her awkwardly on the back.

"Was that when the pain started?"

She nodded. Then, after crying for a while longer, she spoke again.

"The doctor said sometimes a traumatic experience can trigger it. My parents were there, so I didn't say anything, but I think he must have guessed there was something going on, which is why he wants me to see a psychiatrist." She took a deep, shuddering breath. "So I had a grudge against you from the start. I was jealous, I guess. And when you got here, it was so hard to see you treating your dad like that. You had a father who loved you, who wanted you, and you didn't care. But I hope you don't think I was being fake or anything. After our first fight, I really started to understand you better. I started to like you. I'd never thought much about what it would be like to have a sister, but as we got closer, I was genuinely glad you were here.

"And everything was fine. Except my mom was so nice to you, even after how rude you were. And then you met someone, and then she found out she was a bloody *princess*. And what I felt wasn't even jealousy. It just seemed like none of it mattered to you, you know? So at some point I thought . . . maybe you needed a push to finally appreciate all the good things in your life. The things I'd give everything for. That's why I leaked Diana's story. I didn't plan it in advance, but . . . you know that journalist who's obsessed with the royal family?"

I nodded, even though it was a rhetorical question.

"One of my friends is her niece. Kate, who you met at the Tabernacle. And that morning, when you went on your picnic and I had a fight with my mom, I needed to vent. So I decided to call Kate. And then I told her everything." Georgia brought a hand to her forehead. "Deep down, I knew what would happen. But by then it was too late. The truth was already out."

The logical side of me sympathized with Georgia. My chest ached just thinking about how she must have felt after talking with her dad, and then having to put up with me and my anger at the world.

But *damn.*

I was too jittery to stay seated, so I stood up.

"I get that, but did you ever stop to think about how *I* was doing? Your dad told you he never wanted you, which is the worst thing ever, and you must have been devastated. But even though Roberto is welcoming me now, he was a stranger to me for the last ten years. He went to England saying he would give us a better life, and then he just abandoned us. Not only that, he started another family. I understand that he's been an amazing dad to you. But for six-year-old me, it felt like he wanted nothing to do with me. Like he'd quit being my dad."

"You're right," Georgia said quietly.

"And then I lost my mom. My role model, my warrior, the

woman who raised me on her own for more than ten years. So I had to come live with the guy who abandoned me. Do you know how confusing that was? I mean, I'm still confused. Just because I agreed to give Roberto a second chance doesn't mean I'm over it. He hurt me a lot, but I'm willing to give this a try." I took a deep breath, and now I was the one pacing back and forth, trying to control the feelings swirling inside me. "Anyway, I was doing better. I'd met someone awesome, I was getting comfortable with you guys, even starting to see you as my sister." I looked at her, and she burst into tears again. "And you ruined everything."

"I know!" she said more loudly. "I'm so sorry, Day. Please forgive me. I can't undo what I did, but I want you to know that things have been confusing for me, too. I'm also just trying to get through one day at a time."

I felt like my head was about to explode. I had left my anger and hurt feelings behind in Brazil, forgiven myself and apologized to all the people who'd suffered because of me. I'd made up with my friends, talked honestly with my grandparents, and given Roberto a second chance. Georgia was the only one left. And as I listened to her explanation, I realized I couldn't be mad at her. I searched inside myself for the rage that had fueled me the past few months, but it was gone. I didn't want to fight anymore.

I sighed and sat down on the bed. "It's okay."

Georgia dried her nose on the back of her hand. "It's . . . okay?"

I shrugged.

"It's okay," I repeated. "I get it. And I'm tired, I don't want to fight anymore. I left all that behind in Brazil, and I just . . . I just want to start over."

"So you . . . forgive me?" she asked cautiously.

"I can't say it'll be easy to trust you again, but—" I scratched the back of my neck. "I think that's what it means to have a sister, right? My friends and their sisters were constantly arguing and complaining about each other."

I gave her a tired smile, and Georgia smiled back.

She dried her eyes and stared at the floor, tracing patterns on the dark carpet with her finger.

"Thank you, Day. For not giving up on me, too."

Chapter 32

When I woke up the next day, it was still early. So early the house was silent. I poured myself a glass of water and went to sit on the love seat on the back porch. Ruffles poked his head out of his little wooden doghouse and ran over to join me.

One Direction tickets were about to go on sale, and I couldn't risk missing them.

I sat there with my laptop, enjoying the birdsong and the hush of the suburbs, pressing F5 over and over again to refresh the ticket page. The quiet morning felt like a gift. A gift that was even sweeter when I'd made my purchase and gotten my confirmation email. After seven years, I was finally going to see my favorite band live again!

I lost track of time daydreaming about the concert, but at a certain point I heard noise from the kitchen. Lauren must have woken up.

She came out a few seconds later.

"Good morning, querida! I didn't see you out here." She sat down next to me and patted my leg. "Couldn't sleep?"

"Actually, I slept really well for once. I was just buying the tickets for the concert I told you about. By the way . . ." I handed her the credit card I was holding and lowered my voice. "*Thank you.* I promise I'll pay you back."

Lauren smiled, fully aware that I had nothing to base my promise on, since I was likely unemployed. Even so, she'd offered to buy me the tickets without telling Roberto. I'd been talking nonstop about the concert, but I knew it would be too much to ask my dad for help after I'd used his emergency credit card to run away.

"And how was it being back in Brazil?"

"It was hard," I said honestly. "But it was good to see everyone again."

She gave me a little smile, then lowered her head.

"I'm really sorry for what I said," she murmured, and I could tell she was ashamed. "It wasn't your fault, and I shouldn't have blamed you. There's no excuse for saying something like that." She squeezed my hand. "I know I've never been your favorite person, but I want you to know that I'm here to welcome you with open arms and make you feel at home. It won't be the same as your house back in Brazil, of course, and I can never replace your mom, but I hope you'll let me take care of you."

It was the first time I'd heard Lauren make an entire speech without mixing English and Portuguese. It was proof of how serious she was. I smiled shyly.

"I owe you an apology, too. I judged you before I even met

you. I made fun of you, I gave you a nickname . . ." Lauren grimaced, and I bit my lip to stop myself. "Anyway, I thought it was your fault that my dad abandoned me, and when I got here, I couldn't wait to take all my anger out on you. And that wasn't fair."

Lauren squeezed my hand again.

"It was normal for you to feel like that, and in a way, I'm glad to have taken some of the blame. Because that helped protect your relationship with your father. If you'd been angrier at him, it might have been harder to give him a second chance." Lauren sighed, and I thought of all the times I'd misjudged her, before all this happened. I'd been so stupid. She'd never tried to keep me away from my dad. On the contrary. "I disagreed with your father's behavior toward you, and I always encouraged him to be more present. When I met him, things were already falling apart with your mom, but I tried to support him so he could keep the family together. But when I realized their relationship couldn't be salvaged . . . well, there's nothing worse than a broken family that tries to stay together for the 'good' of the children. I know, because I grew up in a house like that. Anyway, I could tell your father felt guilty—he thought nothing he could give you would make up for his absence, but it was still his obligation as a parent. And I did what I could to strengthen your relationship, even if it wasn't that close, because that's what I always wanted from Georgia's father. I still hope that one day he'll have a change of heart and try to meet his incredible daughter."

I thought about what Georgia had told me the night before and looked away. Lauren seemed hopeful, and I felt bad for her. And for Georgia. But maybe it was better to face the hard truth than live with a hope that would never become reality.

She sighed. Then she sat up straight, her energy seemingly restored.

"But you're young, and you have so much ahead of you. You'll love, you'll hate, you'll be angry, and so on. And that's great, as long as you're true to your feelings. Né?" With that, I could tell our serious talk was over. Lauren patted my leg again. "I'll make us some café. Vamos?"

I nodded and stood up, ready to help her in the kitchen. But before she went back inside, she turned around. "What was the nickname you gave me?"

I smiled awkwardly.

"Let's just make some coffee," I said, slipping past her and into the house.

* * *

After breakfast, my dad went upstairs, and the rest of us sat down in the living room to watch TV. That was when Lauren decided it was a good time to update me on the Royal Scandal.

"You missed everything, querida! It's been all gossip all the time," she said gleefully.

I slid down in my seat as images of Rose and Diana being chased by cameras and microphones flashed across the screen.

"Mom . . ." Georgia pleaded with her. She was obviously embarrassed.

"What?" Lauren asked, oblivious to our discomfort. And she chattered on about the royal announcement, which explained how the prince had fathered a child when he was at university but only found out about her recently. "Rumor has it that King Oliver paid them to disappear." She shook her head. "Tsk, tsk. These royals think money solves everything. That woman was right to come back and claim what's hers. And look how pretty her daughter is! A real princess."

A smiling photo of Diana filled the screen, and I felt like I was falling into a bottomless pit.

Up until then, I hadn't stopped to really *think* about her. I'd been mad at her for accusing me, and at myself for having broken my promise. But after all that anger evaporated, I just felt sad.

We'd had so many incredible experiences together, and we'd been there for each other when we needed it most. She'd been my anchor when I was heading straight into the eye of the storm. All the best moments I'd had since my mom's death had been with her.

But as I stared at her face on TV, Diana seemed so far

away. I wanted to find her and apologize and beg for for-
giveness, but the screen in front of me stood between us like
a wall. Who did I think I was to get mixed up with the
prince's daughter?

It was too bold, even for me.

And Lauren was right: She was a real princess.
Apparently, the rumors about Arthur and Tanya's breakup
weren't true, and the royal family had organized an event
at Buckingham Palace. It would be Diana's first official
public appearance, not counting all the times she'd been
ambushed by paparazzi. She was wearing a simple black
spaghetti-strap dress—I could imagine her arguing with
the palace advisors, refusing the gaudy, extravagant outfits favored by the royals—and had taken a no-frills
approach to her hair, which fell in red waves around her
shoulders. Still, she was glowing.

When she smiled, a little hesitantly, the Southern Cross
above her lip shone brighter than stars.

I sighed wistfully.

"You should go there," Georgia said, startling me.

I sat up and looked at her.

"What?" Lauren asked, also turning to her daughter.

Georgia ignored her.

"If you're just going to sit there sulking, you might as well
go apologize and try to win her back."

"Peraí," Lauren said, holding up her hands. "Wait a

minute. *That's* your girlfriend?" She pointed at the TV in disbelief.

I narrowed my eyes at Georgia as if to say *Thanks a lot.* She smiled sheepishly and shrugged.

"Well?" she asked.

I looked away. "Of course I'm not going. They wouldn't even let me in."

"It says it's open to the press until ten. See?" She pointed at the screen. "You just have to take a leap of faith. I believe in you."

"All I can do is text her."

Georgia waved a hand dismissively. "A fight like this calls for a big, dramatic gesture."

I looked back at the journalist who was covering the event on TV.

"Could one of you tell me what's going on?" Lauren asked.

"I'll explain later, Mom," Georgia said, putting a hand on Lauren's arm. "But don't you think Dayana should go after her girlfriend?"

"Claro!" Lauren squealed. She seemed more excited by the fact that my "girlfriend" was Prince Arthur's famous daughter than by the thought of us making up.

But that was okay.

I bit my lip. "Should I?"

"Worst-case scenario, you don't find her." Georgia raised her eyebrows. "You've chased after her for much less."

I tapped my foot nervously. My heart said I should go, but my brain wasn't convinced.

Lauren decided for me. She stood up with so much determination on her face that she could have been the star of an action movie.

"Vamos, meninas. Let's go get Dayana's girl!"

Chapter 33

I smoothed my yellow gingham dress from Primark as the Ford Focus sped down the M25. We turned so sharply onto the exit ramp that I grabbed the ceiling handle.

I gulped, my nerves jangled partly by Roberto's driving and partly by what I was about to do. I still wasn't sure it was a good idea, but Georgia was right. I already had a no, so now all I had to lose was my pride.

As if noticing my anxiety, Georgia reached across the back seat to squeeze my hand. When she smiled, she looked healthy and pain-free.

I'd had a lot of time to reflect in Brazil. As my anger at the world started to ebb, I saw more and more clearly how stupid I'd been not to go after Diana. I'd spent six months dating a boy who was ashamed of me, running after him while he hid me from his friends, trusting him despite all the red flags.

And Diana . . .

Diana had been all green flags from the very beginning. She'd had her secrets, but *I* was never one of them.

My mom always said we should value the people who treat us well, because before we know it, time passes, they're gone, and all that's left is regret. There was a lot I regretted when it came to my mom: the things we hadn't done together, the way I'd treated her, how I hadn't said "I love you" enough. I didn't want Diana to become another regret.

Which is why I was in that car, racing to win back the girl I liked.

I felt like I was living my own version of the end of *Notting Hill*. Except that when I watched the movie, everything felt beautiful and exciting. In real life, I just wanted to throw up.

The car took another sharp turn onto a two-lane road, and my stomach dropped when I saw a double-decker bus coming straight at us.

"Can you remind me why we're in such a rush?" Roberto asked, looking at me in the rearview mirror.

While I was getting changed, Lauren had run around looking for him, shouting that he had to drive us to the palace NOW. None of us had explained what was going on, and I wasn't sure how he'd react.

I took a deep breath.

"I'm going to apologize to the girl I like," I said firmly, my fingers gripping the edge of my seat.

"*WHAT?*" Roberto yelled, turning to look at me.

The car swerved, and the drivers in the other lane blasted their horns. Georgia, Lauren, and I all screamed.

"Eyes on the road, Roberto!" Lauren shrieked, grabbing the steering wheel to keep us in the correct lane.

"But . . . but . . ." he sputtered.

Lauren gave him a pinch on the arm. "But nothing. Just drive."

I felt a wave of gratitude for her. I definitely wasn't ready to have that conversation right now. Or maybe ever.

"Members of the press can go in until ten," Lauren said, checking her watch before glancing at me over her shoulder. "I'm not sure we'll make it."

"Don't worry, we'll figure it out," I said, sounding much braver than I felt.

When we were a block or two away from the palace, Roberto pulled over.

"I need to find somewhere to park," he said, and I leaped from the car without missing a beat.

My legs were literally shaking.

Georgia jumped out on the other side.

"Vai, querida!" Lauren shouted, waving at me through the window. "Good luck!"

As they drove off, Georgia grabbed my hand, and the two of us raced toward one of the side entrances. When I saw that the gates were closed, I bent over with my hands on my thighs, trying to catch my breath. It was 10:15.

What was I going to do?

Calling the place "packed" would have been an understate-
ment. Even though they'd let some of the press in, there
were still hundreds of journalists, tourists, and fans of the
royal family milling around. I was just as curious as they
were, but it would be a lot harder to find a way in with so
many people around.

I could text Diana, but . . . would she respond? Would she
even see it?

I shook my head. No, I'd think of something. I had to see
her face-to-face. It was the only way to find out how she
really felt.

We walked back and forth, looking for an opening.
Nothing came to mind.

"What should we do?" Georgia asked. I scowled at her.

Wasn't she the one who'd told me to take a leap of faith?

A leap of faith. I stopped dead. *That's it.*

I took off running along the palace fence, peeking through
every now and then, hoping to catch a glimpse of her. I
heard Georgia's footsteps close behind. Diana wasn't a huge
fan of the palace, but would she really try to escape again?
She'd only done that before because she was scared to face
the truth. But now that same truth had knocked on her door
and invaded every part of her life. It was stamped on newspapers and magazines all over the country, and maybe the
world.

She didn't have a reason to run anymore.

Even so, my stomach dropped when I reached the place where we'd first met, where the fence gave way to a high wall. There was no one there.

The area was quieter than where we'd been before, but there were still a lot of people around, and reporters were stationed at every entrance. There was no way Diana would try to hop the fence again. They'd catch her.

"I don't know what to do. I've got nothing." I leaned against the fence, gutted.

Georgia paced back and forth in front of me, trying to think. From afar, I saw Roberto and Lauren turn the corner and head toward the crosswalk.

Maybe I should just text her.

But what if she doesn't answer?

I was going through all the options in my head when I heard footsteps on the grass behind me. Instinctively, I pulled Georgia to the side, so we were both hidden behind the wall but still able to see through the fence to the other side.

My heart sped up.

Even before I saw her, I knew it was her.

The sight of her red hair flooded me with happiness. I watched as Diana leaned forward, scanning the crowd. Making sure there was no one nearby. I didn't think she was trying to make a break for it, but maybe this spot had become a refuge where she could stop and take a breath. She seemed lost in the midst of all that attention.

Could everyone else see it, or did I just know her too well? I wasn't sure.

Feeling suddenly fearless, I stepped out from my hiding spot.

"Psst," I whispered, praying the journalists and security guards wouldn't notice.

Diana turned. Her eyes bulged when she saw me, and she came up to the fence, gripping the iron bars.

Standing there in front of her, I forgot everything. All my grief and shame, the guilt that had tortured me for so long, the rage I'd felt. I forgot everything that happened and thought about just one thing: the two of us.

"Dayana? What are you doing here?" she asked, stunned. "I . . . I thought you'd gone back to Brazil."

"I *did* go to Brazil. But I came back."

She hung her head.

"I'm sorry I never answered your text. I didn't want to ruin your life more than I already had. With all this"—she gestured widely, indicating the palace—"I thought you'd be better off without me."

Her sadness surprised me. She hadn't responded because she didn't want to ruin *my* life? Not because she was mad at me?

I took a hesitant step toward the fence.

"I'm the one who should apologize. I was pissed that you didn't trust me, but the real reason I blew up that day was because I was mad at myself. I really shouldn't have told anyone your secret, no matter how much I trusted them." I looked down at my white sneakers. "And in the end, you were right. Georgia *was* the one who told."

I glared at Georgia from the corner of my eye, and she shrank back.

"Sorry," she murmured, retreating a few steps.

Diana shook her head. "It doesn't matter. I shouldn't have taken it out on you. The truth was going to come out sooner or later. I was just so overwhelmed and scared and angry about the whole thing. All at the same time."

"Me too. I was mad at my dad, but also at the whole world. I was so angry that my mom died. And I took that out on you, too."

She laughed quietly, and I took another step forward, wrapping my hands around the iron bars right below hers. A warm, tingly feeling spread through my chest just from being so close to her.

"We were pretty stupid, weren't we?" Diana said, lifting a finger from the bar and stroking my hand. Her touch sent shivers through my whole body, and I couldn't resist taking her hands. "I missed you so much these past few weeks. Everything's been so crazy and intense. Every night when I went to bed, I just wanted to text you, or call you and hear your voice."

My heart fluttered. Then the rest of her words sank in.

"It's been that bad?" I asked anxiously.

She shook her head and smiled.

"No, not really. It's been good. Having my dad. Not hiding anymore. I'm just not crazy about this whole royalty thing." Diana grimaced. "Or being away from you."

I squeezed her hands, and she let out a sigh. Then she looked up at me.

And that was when I saw the first flash. A journalist who had spotted us there at the fence shouted, "The princess!"

Suddenly, a crowd of reporters was running toward us.

Desperation took hold of me.

"They're everywhere, Di!" I looked frantically over my shoulder as they came closer and closer. Roberto and Lauren had crossed the street and were watching us from a few yards away. Georgia stood beside them, taking a video on her phone. I dropped Diana's hands and stepped back. I didn't want to expose her to even more media attention. "We'll talk later. You should go inside, otherwise this could get messy."

But Diana stayed where she was. The journalists clustered around us, flashing their cameras, bombarding us with questions in English.

Diana smiled. "Certain things in life are worth making a mess for. And you're one of them."

I grinned, feeling like the whole world could explode and I

wouldn't even notice. It was just the two of us, like William Thacker and Anna Scott at the end of *Notting Hill*, surrounded by reporters but never taking their eyes off each other.

I stood up straight. This was my moment. As Georgia had said, a fight like ours called for a big, dramatic apology.

In a sudden, wild, head-over-heels rush, I got down on one knee.

Diana's eyes widened through the fence, and cameras flashed all around us. I felt naked. But for her, it was worth it.

"I wanted to say . . ." I declared, looking at Diana and only Diana, "that I'm just a girl, standing in front of *another girl*, asking her to love me."

Diana froze in astonishment. Then she brought her hands to her face, hiding the blush on her cheeks and the radiant smile on her lips.

I stood up, brushing off my knees unglamorously— kneeling had been a *terrible* idea—and leaned toward her.

"What do you say?"

My heart was beating so hard, the reporters' mics were probably catching it. I bit my lip, holding back the stupid smile that threatened to give me away, and raised my eyebrows expectantly.

Diana giggled, and then, to my surprise, she started climbing the fence. I stared at her, dumbstruck by her daring and agility. She pulled herself to the top and looked down at me, eyebrows raised.

I laughed and held out my arms.

Diana jumped.

I obviously couldn't catch her the way I wanted to, and we ended up rolling around on the ground in the most embarrassing moment ever captured on camera.

But none of that mattered.

When Diana propped herself up on her hands and looked at me, I fell headlong into her deep green eyes, which were brimming with happiness.

"I don't know why you'd even ask that," she said, gazing into my eyes. "Can't you tell I already love you?"

She put a hand on my cheek, holding my face so firmly I thought she'd never let go.

But that was okay.

Because I didn't want her to.

She leaned closer, but when our lips were almost touching, I whispered, "I have to tell you something."

Diana drew back slightly, her face curious and a little scared. I almost laughed.

"Did you know One Direction is back?" It took a second for her to realize I'd interrupted our kiss for *this*. "Who's delusional now?" I teased, so euphoric I thought I might burst. Not because I was right or because my favorite band was back together. But because nothing in the world was better than teasing Diana again, laughing with her, touching her.

She sighed and rolled her eyes.

"Oh, shut up," she said. And then she kissed me.

I sighed, too, feeling at peace. The world around us grew silent, and the only thing that existed was Diana, Diana, Diana. Her warm mouth. The taste of nonalcoholic champagne. Her red hair between my fingers. The curve of her waist beneath my hand. The falling stars on her face, answering my greatest wish.

To love and be loved.

Hadn't William Thacker said the chances were always minuscule?

But there I was, in front of the girl with constellations on her skin and a lovestruck smile on her face, looking like she would do anything to make me happy.

And I knew.

I was sure of it.

I was the luckiest girl in the world.

A Queer Icon for the Next Generation

New Lady Di seen kissing girlfriend at Buckingham Palace

Stars Online

Move over, Prince Andrew—there's a new LGBTQIAP+ celeb in the family.

On Saturday, Buckingham Palace welcomed Diana Rose Lima, daughter of Prince Arthur, to her first royal event. And the young princess made quite a splash. In front of a crowd of reporters, Diana received a declaration of love inspired by the classic rom-com *Notting Hill*, then jumped over the palace fence for a passionate kiss with her girlfriend.

Social media is abuzz with commentary, much of it enthusiastic:

YAAAS DIANA! First day as a royal and she's already sticking it to the conservatives #pride

A queer princess?!!! This is everything I needed in my life
Lesbian princess kissing a fat girl I'M OBSESSED
Just because a girl kisses another girl doesn't mean she's a lesbian. STOP BI AND PAN ERASURE. (but also Diana and her gf making out was FIRE)

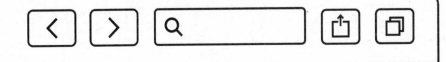

Diana Lima is a pansexual princess. Why does this matter? A thread:
that kiss in front of Buckingham Palace!!! If god hates the gays, WHY DO WE KEEP SLAYING?

But others were less than pleased with Diana's behavior. Multiple sources have reported that the conservative wing of the palace—already in an uproar over the Queen's recent call to review the royal family's diversity policies—may attempt to block a planned proclamation that would grant Arthur's daughter the official title of "princess."

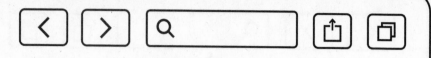

Diana Lima: A Princess at Last

Ignoring critics, Queen grants namesake a royal title

The Daily News

On the 24th of this month, Queen Diana I signed a proclamation guaranteeing the royal title of prince or princess to all the Duke of York's children. As a result, Arthur's illegitimate daughter, Diana Lima, will now officially be addressed as "Your Royal Highness," as will her half brothers, Noah and Sebastian, the sons of Duchess Tanya Parekh.

While the decision came as a blow to the more traditional branch of the monarchy, it was well received by much of the British public. According to a *Daily News* analysis, the royal family's popularity, which was already on the rise following the Queen's coronation, has skyrocketed since the revelation of the younger Diana's existence.

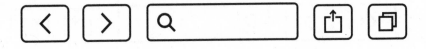

Princess Diana and Girlfriend Spotted at One Direction Reunion Concert

Royal Gossip

What does a princess do on a Friday night? The Duke of York's daughter, for one, spent her evening enjoying a One Direction concert with her girlfriend (the show, held at Wembley Stadium, was the first stop on the boy band's multicity reunion tour). The happy couple was seen holding hands in the crowd, accompanied by several friends. At the end of the night, they visited the band backstage.

The princess's girlfriend, Brazilian Dayana Martins (@daydaym), shared a photo of the couple posing with One Direction, captioned "AAAAAAAAAAAAAAA." Diana replied to the post with a heart and received the following comment in response: "You're the best girlfriend in the world!!!!!"

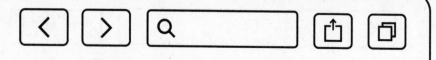

Lady Diana Refuses Royal Title!

by Chloe Ward

Just when we thought we'd seen everything, the royal family announced that Diana Rose Lima has chosen not to accept the royal title of princess.

Trusted sources tell us that the Duke of York's daughter has "no interest in the monarchy or any of that royal nonsense." Queen Diana has apparently not taken kindly to the news, though she herself has been the subject of similar controversies in the past, as when she spoke with the BNC about the discrimination faced by her son, Prince Andrew, who came out of the closet as a teenager.

Every generation, it seems, needs its own Lady Di to challenge the structures of monarchy. As for us, we're looking forward to Diana Rose Lima's next adventure. Even without her title, she'll always be our little princess.

Acknowledgments

London on My Mind didn't come easily. It had so many stages, so many layers. It started in 2018, with the marriage of Prince Harry and Meghan Markle, and my desire to write a fairy tale for everyone who'd never gotten the chance to see themselves in one. Dayana burst into my life like a hurricane: She knew exactly who she was and didn't mind throwing everyone's life—including mine—into chaos.

Maybe that's why it was such a challenge to get this story under control. To find the right tone, the right approach, and above all, the right moment. Between breaks and restructurings and changes of direction, Day finally met Alba Milena and Nathalia Dimambro, who took hold of the novel and helped it become the best version of itself. Alba, thank you for patience with my many emails of IGNORE THE LAST ONE, I CHANGED EVERY-THING, THIS IS THE ONE (it wasn't, of course), as well as my daily freak-outs. I wish I could express how much working with you changed my life. Nati, without your surgical precision, this story would never have gotten on the right track—it would still be chasing its own tail. Thank you for being such a skilled editor. I have full confidence that when readers pick up my books, they're getting the best possible work we could have given them.

A huge thank-you to Marcela Ramos, Sofia Soter, and the whole team at Seguinte for your meticulous eye throughout the editorial process. Truly, I'm so grateful to know that my book was in such capable hands.

A special thank-you to my soul mate, Agatha Machado. You were there from the start, supporting me every step of the way (even the steps backward), cheering me on so fiercely that sometimes it seemed like the book was yours. You have no idea how much I love you. Thank you for being my best friend in the world.

To the Purs, my more-than-perfect support system. I'm so grateful for the laughs, the gossip, and the camaraderie. My life would be so empty without you. Special thanks to Ana Rosa, for your first-rate friendship; to Paula Prata, for being the best assistant ever; to Maria Freitas, for reading this book in advance and making everyone lose their minds about having to wait a year for it; and to Amanda Condasi, for your enthusiasm and advice. When I was a puddle of fear and insecurity, it felt so good to know you all liked this little book.

An enormous thank-you to my mom, Glícia Alves,

for being my number-one fan, and to my whole family, for your love and support.

I can't mention everyone by name, but to all my friends, each of you was and continues to be special not only to my career, but also to my life and personal growth. Having you by my side makes me want to be a better person.

Last but not least, thank you to all my readers—you keep me up at night with your tireless demands for Leo spin-offs and daily messages of *When is your next book coming out, Clara?*, but I love you anyway! Thank you so much for believing in me, following my work, sharing my stories, and asking for more. I've made it so much further than I ever imagined, and it's all thanks to you!

Just like Day, I'm the luckiest girl in the world.

With pride,

Clara

About the Author

Clara Alves has always been passionate about books. She studied journalism and has worked in publishing for years, but she left that all behind to pursue her biggest dream of being a full-time writer. In Brazil, she is the author of the best-selling *Conectadas* and *Romance Real* (published in the US as *London on My Mind*). She lives with her partner in Rio de Janeiro, Brazil.

About the Translator

Nina Perrotta is a literary translator and an editor at Words Without Borders. Her translations from Spanish and Portuguese have appeared in the *Iowa Review* and *The Common*, among other publications. She lives in Oregon.